Sealed with a Hiss

Praise for the Mrs. Murphy Mysteries by Rita Mae Brown and Sneaky Pie Brown:

"As feline collaborators go, you couldn't ask for better than Sneaky Pie Brown."

—*The New York Times Book Review*

"Enchanting . . . Brown demonstrates once again why she's the queen of the talking animal cozy subgenre."

—*Publishers Weekly*

"[Brown] successfully weaves mystery, history, real estate and romance. . . . The blend is unusual but gripping, and combined with bipedal and quadrupedal characters who constitute old friends, it shines as imaginative and educational entertainment."

—*Richmond Times-Dispatch*

"This engaging series remains fresh."

—Fredericksburg *Free Lance–Star*

"Fun and satisfying . . . an essential purchase for all mystery collections."

—*Booklist*

"Clearly the cat's meow."

—*Library Journal*

Books by Rita Mae Brown & Sneaky Pie Brown

WISH YOU WERE HERE • REST IN PIECES • MURDER AT MONTICELLO • PAY DIRT
MURDER, SHE MEOWED • MURDER ON THE PROWL • CAT ON THE SCENT
SNEAKY PIE'S COOKBOOK FOR MYSTERY LOVERS • PAWING THROUGH THE PAST
CLAWS AND EFFECT • CATCH AS CAT CAN • THE TAIL OF THE TIP-OFF
WHISKER OF EVIL • CAT'S EYEWITNESS • SOUR PUSS • PUSS 'N CAHOOTS
THE PURRFECT MURDER • SANTA CLAWED • CAT OF THE CENTURY
HISS OF DEATH • THE BIG CAT NAP • SNEAKY PIE FOR PRESIDENT
THE LITTER OF THE LAW • NINE LIVES TO DIE • TAIL GAIT • TALL TAIL
A HISS BEFORE DYING • PROBABLE CLAWS • WHISKERS IN THE DARK
FURMIDABLE FOES • CLAWS FOR ALARM • HISS & TELL • FELINE FATALE
SEALED WITH A HISS

Books by Rita Mae Brown featuring "Sister" Jane Arnold

OUTFOXED • HOTSPUR • FULL CRY • THE HUNT BALL
THE HOUNDS AND THE FURY • THE TELL-TALE HORSE • HOUNDED TO DEATH
FOX TRACKS • LET SLEEPING DOGS LIE • CRAZY LIKE A FOX • HOMEWARD HOUND
SCARLET FEVER • OUT OF HOUNDS • THRILL OF THE HUNT • TIME WILL TELL
CLAWED AND DANGEROUS

The Mags Rogers Books

MURDER UNLEASHED • A NOSE FOR JUSTICE

Books by Rita Mae Brown

ANIMAL MAGNETISM: MY LIFE WITH CREATURES GREAT AND SMALL
THE HAND THAT CRADLES THE ROCK • SONGS TO A HANDSOME WOMAN
A PLAIN BROWN RAPPER • RUBYFRUIT JUNGLE • IN HER DAY • SIX OF ONE
SOUTHERN DISCOMFORT • SUDDEN DEATH • HIGH HEARTS
STARTED FROM SCRATCH: A DIFFERENT KIND OF WRITER'S MANUAL • BINGO
VENUS ENVY • DOLLEY: A NOVEL OF DOLLEY MADISON IN LOVE AND WAR
RIDING SHOTGUN • RITA WILL: MEMOIR OF A LITERARY RABBLE-ROUSER

Sealed with a Hiss

RITA MAE BROWN &
SNEAKY PIE BROWN

Illustrated by Michael Gellatly

BANTAM BOOKS
NEW YORK

Bantam Books
An imprint of Random House
A division of Penguin Random House LLC
1745 Broadway, New York, NY 10019
randomhousebooks.com
penguinrandomhouse.com

2026 Bantam Books Trade Paperback Edition

Originally published in hardcover in the United States by Bantam Books, an imprint of Random House, a division of Penguin Random House LLC, in 2025.

ISBN 978-0-593-87410-3
Ebook ISBN 978-0-593-87409-7

Printed in the United States of America on acid-free paper

1st Printing

BOOK TEAM: Production editor: Andy Lefkowitz • Managing editor: Saige Francis • Production manager: Jennifer Backe • Copy editor: Pam Feinstein • Proofreaders: Kate Hertzog, Allison Lindon, and Robin Slutzky

Book design by Diane Hobbing

The authorized representative in the EU for product safety and compliance is Penguin Random House Ireland, Morrison Chambers, 32 Nassau Street, Dublin D02 YH68, Ireland. https://eu-contact.penguin.ie

To Hugh H. Brown, III, MFH
Working with you has been a joy.

CAST OF CHARACTERS

Mary Minor Haristeen, "Harry," was the postmistress of Crozet right out of Smith College. As times changed and a big new post office was built, new rules came, too, such as she couldn't bring her animals to work, so she retreated to the farm she inherited from her parents. Born and raised in Crozet, she knows everyone and vice versa. She is now forty-five, although one could argue whether maturity has caught up with her.

Pharamond Haristeen, DVM, "Fair," is an equine vet specializing in reproduction. He and Harry have known each other all their lives. They married shortly after she graduated from Smith and he was in vet school at Auburn. He generally understands his wife better than she understands herself.

Susan Tucker is Harry's best friend from cradle days. They might as well be sisters and can sometimes pluck each other's last nerve as only a sister can. Susan bred Harry's adored corgi. Her husband, Ned, is the district's delegate to the General Assembly's House of Delegates, the lower house.

Deputy Cynthia Cooper is Harry's neighbor, as she rents the adjoining farm. Law enforcement is a career she is made for, being meticulous, shrewd, and highly observant. She works closely with the sheriff, Rick Shaw; adores Harry; and all too often has to extricate her neighbor out of scrapes. Harry returns the favor by helping Coop with her garden. It probably isn't an equal exchange but they are fine with it.

Tazio Chappers is an architect in her late thirties, born and raised in St. Louis. Having been educated at Washington University, she received an excellent education, winding up in Crozet on a fluke. Just one of those things, as Cole Porter's song lets us know. Warned off a job at an architectural firm by many people back in Missouri, due to her being half Black and half Italian, she came to Virginia, anyway. No one can accuse her of being a chicken. Now owner of her own firm, getting big jobs, she is happy, married for two years, and part of the community. She is also terrifically good-looking, which never hurts.

Lucas Harkness helps Aunt Tally on her farm and lives in a small cottage on her estate. He wears many hats: secretary, campaign planner, willing ear. He loves her deeply but is not in love with her.

Miranda Hogendobber worked with Harry for years at the old post office. In her early eighties she knows everyone and she herself is well-known for her beautiful singing voice.

Aunt Tally, who is now 103, has become frail. Her mind is very good, only her body is slowing down. Given the harsh winter, she is lonely and snowbound. Harry drops in on her. There is not one person in Crozet who knows life without Aunt Tally.

Sandy Rycroft is the owner and head broker of Hickory Real Estate, which he inherited from his father.

Armand Neff does business around the world. Jovial and generous, he proves helpful in the celebration of the restored schools.

Moses Evenfall went through the schools, becoming the baseball and football coach.

Sherry Tutweiler married Coach Evenfall. They have been married almost seventy years. She was a History teacher.

THE ANIMALS

Mrs. Murphy is Harry's tiger cat. She is bright, does her chores, keeps the mice at bay when need be. Harry talks to her but not baby talk. Mrs. Murphy just won't have it.

Pewter is fat, gray, and vain, oh so vain. She irritates Tucker, the corgi. She takes credit for everyone else's work. However, in a pinch the naughty girl does come through. She's also quite bright.

Tee Tucker, the corgi bred by Susan Tucker, runs around everyone. She's fast, loves to greet every person once she has checked them out, and particularly likes to herd the horses. The horses are good sports about it, which is excellent. Tucker is brave and she loves Harry totally.

Pirate is a not-yet-fully-grown Irish Wolfhound who landed in Harry's lap as a puppy when his owner died. Huge, able to cover so much ground, he can be dominated by Pewter sometimes. Tucker has to give him pep talks. Like Tucker, Pirate has great courage and loves being part of the family. He is trying to understand people. The others help. A sweet, sweet animal.

The mice at the schools lead a good life.

Sealed with a Hiss

PROLOGUE

Mother Nature exercises ultimate power. She can push up mountains or tear them down. She can create drought, flooding, epidemics, pathways to healing. Humans live at her mercy.

Swift Creek courses through Albemarle County. The current rolls along; in places, the creek is remarkably deep. During a hard flood those formerly sparkling waters can tear down a bridge and carry huge trees, only to deposit them in a pasture.

Recent hard rains caused damage throughout the county. People had experienced worse but cleanup takes time, no matter the extent of the damage.

Swift Creek holds an undiscovered car, sunken since 2006. Trapped behind the steering wheel rests a man's remains.

All those years ago he was murdered. He would be found, shocking those who discovered him.

Dead all those years, what was his secret? Who could it affect today?

1

May 4, 2024

Saturday

Everything happens in the kitchen.

Harry swatted her fat gray cat off the windowsill behind the kitchen sink. Pewter, the offending feline, was cussing the bluejay who was attacking the window with ferocious screeches. These two have hated each other for years. Harry couldn't decide if this was Methusalah's bluejay or progeny from the original pair who had nested high in the large walnut tree.

"Will you stop this racket?"

"*It's not me. I didn't start it,*" Pewter defended herself, not that Harry understood what was coming out of the fanged mouth.

However, Harry did grasp Pewter's emotions.

Flopped on the kitchen floor, sprawled on the beautiful uneven pine, Mrs. Murphy, the tiger cat, lifted her head then dropped it. No point to get involved.

Tee Tucker, the corgi, took this opportunity to smart off about Pewter. "*She has no sense. She'll never get that bluejay.*"

"Shut up, fat butt. I will kill that bird. I only need the chance." The gray cat spit.

"Ha."

Before Harry could advise her dog to keep quiet, Pewter launched off the windowsill, touched the countertop once, then sailed onto the recumbent dog. Sounded like the end of the world.

"That's enough." Harry knew enough not to smack either one of them. Instead she grabbed for the duster hanging on the wall and tickled both with the feathers. It broke them apart.

Mrs. Murphy moved away the minute Pewter landed on Tucker.

"We should stick together," the tiger cat advised the young Irish Wolfhound, Pirate.

Not quite two, still learning human ways, the huge fellow sat up just in case he needed to run out of the room. With the gray cat and the corgi, one was never certain if the fury would spread.

"Right." Pirate loved Mrs. Murphy.

Harry shook the feathers over the combatants again. "I mean it. You two stop it. Right now."

Tucker, now on her feet, glanced up at Harry's face, realizing her two-legged friend meant it. She moved away from the cat.

"I knew you were afraid of me." Pewter puffed up.

Tucker curled up her lip, growled.

"Tucker. Forget it." Then Harry turned to the preening cat. "Don't be so full of yourself."

"Susan." Tucker shot away, blasted through the animal door in the kitchen door, to the outside porch.

"Gave her an excuse to run." Pewter licked her paw, rubbing it on her dark gray face.

"I wouldn't tangle with you," Pirate honestly said, which puffed up Pewter even more.

The kitchen door opened, Susan stepping through it, Tucker right behind her.

"Is this rain ever going to stop? You know, there are flood warnings again."

Harry walked over to the stove, flicked on the flame under the teapot. "Sit down. Or you can pull the corn bread out of the fridge, plus butter."

"Your corn bread is the best."

"Coming from you, that's praise, but I think Aunt Tally's is the best." Harry smiled at her oldest friend, from cradle days.

"She's had a longer time to perfect it." Susan laughed, as Aunt Tally was one hundred and three.

Now in their early forties, both women tried to ignore the passing years, but a little sag here, an errant ache there sounded the warning. "Time is flying."

Corn bread, plates, butter, and two cups of fabulous Assam tea graced the table as the two sat down.

"These animals are driving me crazy. One fight after another. Mostly Pewter and Tucker, but still, rainy days get on everyone's nerves. Not so much on mine."

"Given how much you overseeded last fall, I would think not." Susan smiled. "Ned and I thought about overseeding the front lawn. Decided to wait to see if prices fell in the spring. You know the argument about seeding in spring versus seeding in late fall. I remember when you bought all that orchard grass seed."

"Me too." Harry took a long sip of her tea, the temperature perfect. "The news keeps saying inflation is falling. Well, honeybunch, I don't see it. Went to Harris Teeter yesterday. Three bags of groceries, $198. The only expensive item in there were two T-bone steaks. Yes, gas has slipped down a bit, but I sure don't see it for food. Thank God it's warming up. I don't see my electric prices falling either."

"No."

"Sorry, here I am bitching and moaning. You know I'm glad to see you. I'm always glad to see you."

Susan grinned. "Same here. I've brought my notes for the school celebration. The weekend after Memorial Day will be here before we know it." She reached into her back jean pocket, retrieving a small notebook.

"You were never born with a notebook in your hand. In History class I'd be furiously scribbling and you'd jot down a word or a date. God, I used to think Mr. Spencer would never shut up."

Susan nodded. "The world is full of Mr. Spencers."

Remembering to fetch her notebook, Harry rose, walked into the library, plucked her large notebook off a desk, returned, sat down with two pens she'd also taken from the desk. She rolled one over to Susan. "Fire away."

Susan tapped the pen on the table. "Coach Evenfall gives the closing speech after Evie Rogers, valedictorian of the class of 1959."

The term *colored school* was used throughout Virginia. Walter Ashby Plecker, a physician, became the registrar of the Bureau of Vital Statistics. He believed in racial categories and pushed through the Racial Integrity Act in 1924. People of the Virginia tribes were lumped in the same category as Black people, under the term "colored" people, a label that was harmful to all of them.

Public schools had been segregated in Virginia since 1870 but now the screening was more stringent.

This act prevented numerous tribes from receiving Federal recognition until 1984. A few remain unrecognized.

Harry, Susan, Ned, Fair, Tazio, and lately Lucas Harkness had worked to keep the physical schools in Crozet from destruction. Tazio, herself mixed race, started this eight years ago.

The dedication of the restored buildings was to be after Memorial Day. Those who had gone before would be honored.

Harry, spiral notebook fully opened, remarked, "Isn't Tazio going to open everything? Then she introduces Moses Evenfall?"

"The mayor, then Tazio. We know Taz will stick to her time restriction. Will Coach and Mrs. Rogers and Norton Sessions?"

"We don't know." Harry twirled her pen. "Many of the guests will have gone to school with those two, but most of our guests from that time will only have been in the lower grades. There are fewer and fewer of those who graduated from high school in the fifties. We've received twenty replies, many out of state from the older students. You know who probably is familiar with some of the older people is Aunt Tally." Harry cited the corn-bread queen.

"She might, but she's white, obviously, so she went to a different school."

"But people knew one another. Same community, so despite the divide of race, everybody knew everybody. That's what my mother used to say when she'd admonish me to remember my manners."

Susan sighed. "I guess. Are you saying Aunt Tally might have an idea about a speaker getting overly chatty?"

"I'm not very worried. Each keynote speaker has ten minutes. That's actually a long time when you add it up." Harry looked down at Pewter, fast asleep from her drama's drain of energy.

"You forgot politicians." Susan's husband was a member of the Virginia House of Delegates from District 57.

"Fortunately, except for a few remarks from the mayor of Crozet, we have no politicians. Also the mayor is Jim Sanburne. He's in his eighties now. His wife, Mim, will never tolerate a drawn-out speech."

"That's the truth." Susan laughed as Big Mim Sanburne really ran Crozet. "I figure fifty-five minutes total. Someone always runs over."

"You know what? I will talk to Aunt Tally." Harry took a deep breath. "Her mind is so good. She said last time we spoke that she'll be at the event."

"It's wonderful that she wants to be part of this." Susan adored the old lady, as did most people. No one knew Crozet without her. "What about the Walter Plecker flyer? We proofread it but it's not published yet. Not everyone knows the history of the schools of Virginia."

"One thousand copies. I still think we could have gotten by with five hundred."

"We could, but big printing is so much cheaper per copy, and when the school year starts we'll have plenty for those who want them. Don't start fretting about money. It's too late." Susan rapped Harry's hand with her pen.

"It's frightening how one man in 1912 could do so much damage for so many decades." Susan added, "Those flyers are important. Plecker made it worse in 1924, 1930. In 1912 he focused on birth certificates. Until then records were in family Bibles."

"Our history is important whatever century. Sure gets twisted, though, by people trying to pump up careers or make money off other people's suffering." Harry loathed those people.

"Harry, it never ends. There were hypocrites in the Roman Senate, Athens, every government, it's part of human nature."

A long sigh escaped Harry's lips. "You know, that's why I love my animals. They're honest."

Tucker couldn't resist. "*Pewter pretends to be starving when she isn't. She also opens the cabinet doors and blames it on the rest of us.*"

"*I do not. Plus, I open the cabinet doors to see if there are treats, and you eat those treats. Don't deny it. I have pulled out treats and you ate them.*"

"*You tore open the bags.*" Tucker didn't like the direction this discussion was taking.

Harry, hearing the chat, the tone of the voices, leaned down. "No fighting. I am tired of you two."

They blinked innocently.

Mrs. Murphy whispered to Pirate, "*Let's just say, they can both eat.*"

"*Are you talking about me?*" Pewter raised her voice.

Mrs. Murphy replied, whiskers forward, "*Why would we be talking about you?*"

Without hesitation Pewter answered, "*Because I'm fascinating.*"

"*I'm going to be sick.*" Tucker gagged.

Harry got up, opened the door to the screened-in porch. "Out. Tucker, out."

With sorrowful eyes, her devoted dog slowly moved to the door. Of course, she wasn't sick.

"*Ha,*" Pewter triumphed.

"Come to think of it, you all go outside for a bit. Now."

Pirate walked out first after Tucker then Mrs. Murphy, with Pewter dragging at the rear. No sooner were the animals out in the refreshing spring air than the bluejay dive-bombed Pewter.

Harry, still up, looked out the window over the sink. Susan, hearing the screech, stood up to look out the kitchen sink window, too.

"It never ends. Drives me crazy," Harry moaned, then laughed.

"Let's hope our opening of the school is calmer than your house."

"It will be. Who could dive-bomb us?"

2

May 5, 2024

Sunday

Moses Evenfall, one leg over the other, propped his clipboard on his crossed knee.

His wife, Sherry, washing lettuce, turned to look at him. "Honey, it's not the State of the Union address."

He smiled. "Well, it is to me."

She took her walker, next to the sink, and made her way to him, kissing him on the cheek. "You'll have them eating out of your hand. Think of all those speeches you gave at halftime to the football team."

He reached for her hand, now off the walker. "Not the same."

"Well, you're a good public speaker."

"Well . . ." His voice trailed off as she sat next to him in a comfortable chair.

"You have quite a bit of time."

"I know, but I want to get this right. Short and sweet, want to memorize it. I'm not standing in front of all those people with papers in my hand."

"That means you'll practice on me." She lifted an eyebrow.

"Yes." He smiled.

"Has Tazio mentioned how many people might be there?"

"From both schools, we've got about two hundred total. Not so many from the high school. Most of the grade-schoolers are now in their sixties, seventies. From the local community, not school graduates, there's no way to know. But Taz and that group will have extra chairs, drinks. You know how organized they are," Moz said.

"Yes. Harry, Susan, Fair, Ned, some of their friends, and Jerry Showalter. He got all the old books, remember? They've been working on this for years. Plus they raised the money."

"We're lucky that Jim Sanburne is the mayor or this could have been stopped. Not everyone wants to see that land off the market."

"True. Jim faced down the county commissioners when they stepped in declaring the sum those twenty acres could bring. It's not about the money." Sherry recalled how hard Jim had fought.

"If you're a politician, it's usually about the money." He lifted his clipboard off his knee. "Nobody wanted the place until it got fixed up."

"Be a fool to cross a Sanburne, any Sanburne." She took the clipboard from his hand. " 'We might give out, but we won't give up.' " She looked at him. "That's an unusual start."

"That's what I always said to my football teams, but it applies to the dedication of the group that's saved the school, restored those three buildings. And you know, it's not a bad motto for those of us who attended, who graduated, who made our way in the world the best we could at the time."

"Mmm. You'll do a wonderful job, sweetheart. I know you will. Plus, my handsome husband, eighty-seven and you look just like you did when you coached, except your hair is white."

"Keep moving. You keep moving." He squeezed her hand. "Speaking of never giving up."

"I feel a little better every day. You know we're old. What's going to get us in the end? Stroke, heart attack, or cancer. Well, I had my stroke.

Going to take more than that." She laughed. "But really. My daily walks help. And you still do your exercises plus your two-mile walk."

"I could lose a few pounds, and I mean to lose them by speech time. I've lost ten. Another five."

"Do you think we'll recognize the people who've come from far away? Tazio said Bertha Bass is coming from California and your best halfback will be flying in from Chicago, Bobby Underhill. When you think of how small our school was and yet how many boys you got into college even in those days. Football, baseball, basketball."

"Those kids were good. The girls, too. Boy, do I ever remember Tillie Fountain. At football practice one day, she came to watch her boyfriend. He threw her the ball. She passed it sixty yards right into the arms of the receiver. I almost passed out."

"She wound up teaching pro golf at the city course, as you know. Think where she'd be today? And then to die of breast cancer before forty. Honest to God, you never know."

"No, you don't," he agreed.

"Well, let me get back to supper. Salad. I don't think you need to lose weight but if you declare five more pounds, then five more pounds it will be. And my goal is no walker on the day."

She rose to go back to the lettuce. He watched her, proud of her. He wondered why she said yes to him sixty-five years ago. She could have had anyone. Sixty-five years of love, laughter, happiness; what a home run.

While Sherry Evenfall was making salad, Tazio, Harry, and Susan sat in Tazio's light-filled office.

"What I did was order food, easy stuff: chicken, salad, mac and cheese, hamburgers, all the usual for four hundred people. That should do it," Tazio told them. "How we'll pay for this is another issue."

"People in the community have filled out their invitation card.

My fear is that people are just going to walk in," Harry said, also worried about costs.

"Some will. But it shouldn't be overwhelming," Susan replied. "We have security, TV, and the *Richmond Times Dispatch*."

"I'll check with Reverend Jones, he's good with backup plans," Harry promised. "I just hope it doesn't rain. I keep checking long-range forecasts. Looks good."

"All these years. All the work and now we're here." Tazio reflected for a moment. "It's hard to believe."

The other two agreed.

Two knocks on the door, then Lucas Harkness opened it from outside, bent over, picked up a cooler, and joined the meeting. "I've got everything you like."

They rose as he plopped the cooler on the floor, opening the lid. "Good news. Armand Neff agreed to talk to me about the food bill," Lucas said.

Harry grabbed an iced tea, Susan picked out a light beer, and Tazio rubbed her fingers over an ice-cold bottle of Perrier. Everyone picked a cup, filled it with ice cubes, then sat back down. Harry, sitting next to Lucas, put her hand on his forearm. "We'll all say our prayers about Armand."

"Beer?" Tazio looked at Susan. "I don't remember you drinking beer, especially in the late afternoon."

"Well, I've gotten into the habit. A light beer, really cold. I'm trying to wean off sugary drinks and if I drink an iced tea after five, then I won't sleep."

"I'll have to try it." Tazio smiled. "So, Lucas, flowers?"

"The Unitarian Church, St. Mary's, and First Presbyterian have promised that their ladies guilds will do the flowers. There will be various tables; as you know, we're not having formal tables except up front for speakers. Also tables in the classrooms. We'll have small arrangements, give this some color, celebrate spring." He took a breath. "And the best part is people can buy them when the dedication is over."

"Good idea." Susan nodded. "One can never have enough flowers."

"Western Albemarle?" Harry inquired about the high school band in the western part of the county, right outside Crozet.

"They'll get everyone focused, as they'll begin the show, as it were. March right up the driveway."

"In their colors?" Tazio inquired about the marching band.

"Yes," Lucas responded.

"Is anyone wearing the Colored School colors?" Susan wondered. "Feels wrong to call it the Colored School, when we wouldn't call it that anymore."

"I think some people will wear school colors. Their colors were purple and gold and that's what we have as the decorations, as well as the ribbons around the flowerpots. Should be pretty. Boy, don't you wish we had their old marching band?" Tazio grinned. "Everyone who ever heard them said they were the best, best, best.

"Any gossip or concern about impromptu speeches?" Tazio had a backup plan in case.

"Not that I've heard, but you know Moz Evenfall will take care of anything. No one will fool around with him." Susan had known the coach her whole life, as had many people in Crozet.

"I hope that's true. Lots of the graduates still living will be here. It's going to be an emotional day for all of us, I think." Tazio grasped her cold cup, felt good.

"Any advice on crying babies?" Harry suddenly remembered how loud babies could be.

"Oh, the mothers will walk them away. I'm not worried." Tazio felt confident.

"Dogs barking?" Lucas wondered.

"There's bound to be a yip and a yap but those noises can be controlled or reduced. That's why part of the food is dog biscuits. You know people will want to walk their dogs. They walk them around the schools now. The first time I saw a couple with their dachshund, I was surprised." Tazio then added, "But I realized the place was becoming attractive. Good for dogs. Good for people."

"Lucas, heard anything about real estate companies sniffing out the school's land?" Harry asked him, as when he was a secretary in the House of Delegates he'd had a lot of contact with large real estate companies.

"No. Last year Thanatos seemed to be interested. I know they contacted the commissioner of the district. Jim Sanburne got wind of it. He apparently shut that down. But so far, nothing really."

"The grounds are twenty acres plus a yard or two. I wouldn't let down our defenses." Harry never trusted developers. "A large company can make a case for taking that land at a big price, music to the County Commission's ears. They develop a community using the schools as a theme yet being far enough away from the buildings themselves. I'm not saying it's going to happen, but when you think of the money that could be made, and the old argument that everyone will benefit from those real estate tax dollars, that can sway people."

"It's not going to happen at the celebration." Tazio was firm. "Afterward, who knows? Crozet is expanding faster than I ever imagined and for you all who were born and raised here, it has to be unsettling. Really, could you afford your own house today or your farm, Harry?"

"No," Harry replied.

"Probably not," Susan joined in.

"Well, as I have been looking for a house, I can testify to how difficult it now is." Lucas finished his drink. "It's going to take luck. I don't want to take Aunt Tally for granted." He lived in a dependency at Aunt Tally's estate.

"Maybe everything takes luck." Harry smiled. "You know I'm relieved you're over there. Her great-niece and family travel so much."

They went over some more details, such as leashes to buy should anyone lose one, stuff like that, and then the meeting slid into visiting among friends.

Always the best.

3

May 6, 2024

Monday

For early May, the day proved unusually cool. The mercury stuck at 60 degrees. Harry walked behind the old school buildings, the two cats and two dogs enjoying the walk, something different from home. Given the years Harry had worked on this restoration, they'd been to the schoolhouse in all weather, each learning how efficient those old woodburning stoves were in the winter.

A creek, about ten feet wide and maybe four feet deep—shallow, for the most part—ran at the western edge of the property. Central Virginia was laced with creeks, larger branches leading to rivers, those rivers flowing to larger rivers until winding up in one of the great rivers enriching the state; Potomac, Rappahannock, the James flowing ultimately to the sea. Virginia had beaches, flatlands, rolling hills up to the Blue Ridge and the Appalachians. Only a desert was missing, and no one seemed to mind. The Chesapeake Bay, shared with Maryland, was another distinctive draw.

As Harry walked along in her work boots, the footing was soft, the grass already green and growing. This all needed to be bush-hogged before the event. She would do it, as she owned two tractors, one midsize, one 85 horsepower, both had bush-hogs to do the cutting. She should be able to knock out the mowing in two hours, give or take, as one never knows what one will find, hence her walking as much as she could today. Fair could later weedwack. She hated weedwacking and edging. So she decided to mow all by herself. She'd brought bright-colored tape to mark downed limbs already hidden by grass.

Tucker, who knew the land well, ran alongside the creek bed. *"Hey, new ford."*

Pirate ran over to examine this. The cats stayed with Harry, following in her footsteps as she trod down the grass. Made it easier for them.

Tucker continued to bark, so Harry walked to see what the noise was about.

Reaching her intrepid corgi, she immediately noticed the new ford.

"Every time it floods, this creek changes a bit."

Something glittering in the loam a foot off the creek bank caught her interest. She put one foot in the water. The work boots once were waterproof, but now old, if she stayed in the water too long her feet would get wet. Bending over, she pushed away the wet sand, plucking out a belt buckle.

She turned it over in her hand. It was old, had "U.S." on the front, but she had no way of knowing *how* old it was. She stepped back on land, her feet still dry, and noticed a few odd quartz rocks, which she felt was always a sign of water, including underground streams. She picked up one, noticed a bluestone about four inches long with bright speckles next to it. Pocketed that, too.

Within fifteen minutes she reached the back of the three identical school buildings. The wooden rectangular buildings were built to last, and so they did. Originally they had no electric, nor did anyone else at the time. The restoration project upgraded to later plumbing and electricity needs. The structures were solid. The floor-to-ceiling windows, which had very large panes, took money to replace. Over the years vandals had broken some. When the group took this on, that was the first thing they did, followed by cleaning the chimneys. The stoves, never tampered with, were fired up in each building. Worked. The first time Tazio, Susan, and Harry tested them on a surprisingly cold late September day, they cheered, as the room heated quickly in the grade school building. They trooped over to the high school, identical to the grade school, cranked up that woodstove. Again, noticeable warmth within fifteen minutes. They'd work on that space later. The two big classroom buildings reached the mid-sixties within forty-five minutes. The three women sat, each one in an old school desk, happy to sit down, happy to remove their coats. Harry's pets felt happy, too.

Throughout Virginia, all of these schools were called the Colored Schools. The restoration committee would not fool with the state's distinctive history but they were happy to hear the old graduates wanted to rename them for an as-of-yet unselected person.

On that first cold day came Susan's notebook, as she jotted down what wood they put into the stove, what kindling, how long it took to warm the entire space. Of course, the farther away one was from the stove, the cooler it would be, but it wasn't bad.

That cheered them. Sitting there talking, happy to be warm, they looked out the fabulous windows as leaves twirling down off trees gave them energy. They now believed they could bring the schools back to life. No throttling history, no letting everyday lives fade away.

Looking at the tidy front of the building as Harry walked she remembered the hours spent, the years of work begging, borrowing, scrubbing, researching, the little victories. Funny how when one is immersed in a passion, time is a blur. Throughout her life Harry had been involved at St. Luke's Lutheran, especially taking care of the grounds, the old roof. Doing church maintenance, working her farm, helping out Aunt Tally at her farm, she kept busy. Harry's favorite charity was Guide Dogs for the Blind. She didn't have the wherewithal to write big checks for the guide dogs, but she would raise a bit of money once a year, through her friends. That and the schools turned out to be the projects closest to her heart.

"Come on, a quick check." She took out her key, unlocked the door to the grade school. The door opened without a squeak. The hinges were oiled up once a week, worked as though new. Stepping through the threshold, she then stopped. Coolish but not cold, the one room sparkled. The teacher's desk, raised on a dais, gleamed. They'd rubbed it with lemon oil, put an old mug with pencils on the right-hand side, a few schoolbooks on the left. In the center was a leather pad, a letter opener, a letter holder stuffed with letters from earlier times, those canceled stamps announcing the year plus the cost of a first-class letter. If one opened the center drawer, dated lesson plans rested within.

The group tried to make the interior look as though the students were just gone for the weekend. Each desk had been cleaned, polished, the top easy to lift again, 3-in-One Oil to the rescue.

The floor had been waxed and polished, as it had been once a week since day one. They hoped the returning students would feel as though they had stepped back in time.

"Mice behind the teacher's desk," Mrs. Murphy announced.

"I'll dispatch them," Pewter bragged.

This was bull, but Tucker piped up, *"You can't do that because they are the descendants of the original mice. Plus, they aren't going to come out with all the activity."*

"Won't the people smell them?" Pirate asked.

"All that the humans will smell is lemon oil. And really, the mice don't smell bad. You need to remember, Pirate, humans have terrible noses. Poor things." Tucker appeared sympathetic.

Mrs. Murphy hopped up on the dais, circling the desk. Pewter followed. The dogs followed Harry as she walked along the far aisle, checking the storage door and the bathroom door, making certain they were locked.

"Clever." Mrs. Murphy, now under the desk, which sat high, inspected a wide leg. The mice had chewed through it, making enough room to hide if necessary.

"I bet there's a way down; they've chewed through the floor. No one can see the hole obviously, and they can walk along the space under the floor." Pewter then added, *"If there isn't a space between the top of the floor and a bottom set of boards, then there's a pole, somewhere they climb up and down."*

"This floor was in good shape when Mom started restoring the buildings. So either they added another layer with insulation in between, or you're right, there has to be a pole or something so they can come in through the basement. We've never been down there. But if a mouse scurries out, I bet people will scream." Mrs. Murphy laughed.

"We'd better make sure to be at the big party." Pewter felt certain they could handle any mishap.

"Come on," Harry called as she opened the door to check the high school building.

The two cats hurried out.

"What's so interesting?" Tucker asked.

"The mice in the grade school don't have a hole in the wall. It's in the back leg of the desk. You can't see it, it's on the inside, not anything that shows outside. We don't know what's underneath. There has to be some way they can climb up," Mrs. Murphy informed the dogs.

"Well, if they're smart, they'll stay put," Tucker said.

"Maybe they have a sense of humor." Pewter walked through the open door to the high school building.

"Do mice have a sense of humor?" Pirate was baffled.

"All animals have a sense of humor," Tucker vowed. *"Maybe reptiles don't but consider Matilda. She certainly has one."*

"Python." Pewter spit.

Matilda was the large black snake who wintered in the basement at the farm. She usually wrapped around one of the pipes under the sink. She'd emerge during spring to hang on branches of the walnut tree. If the black snake flicked her tongue out, it made Pewter men-

tal. The bluejay was bad enough. The large snake once allowed Harry to pick her up before an outdoor luncheon. Harry couldn't believe how heavy the big girl was. She put Matilda back in the basement for good measure. The black snake emerged as soon as the last guest drove down the farm road.

Harry walked through the high school building. Everything checked out. One wall had bookcases. The books had been published before the schools were closed. Jerry Showalter found all of them. Many of the old spines still glittered with silver or gold lettering.

Harry pulled *My Bondage and My Freedom* by Frederick Douglass, opened it, and marveled at how dark the ink was on the pages, no cheap paper. The letters had been cut into the paper so the edges, sharp, never looked a tiny bit blurry, as modern books do. She closed it, replacing it on the shelf.

"Okay. All looks presentable."

"Hey, a mouse hole in this teacher's desk, too," Pewter noted.

They walked out, Harry locked the front door, stepped away from the three buildings, looked over a pasture to the left and south of them. She walked toward the end of it, maybe a quarter mile, turned, walked back.

"I don't know," she mumbled.

"Now what?" Pewter was ready to go home.

Harry pulled her cellphone out from her back pocket, hit a speed dial. "Susan."

"You're at the school, aren't you?"

"Well, yes." Harry shrugged.

"I knew you couldn't help yourself. What's wrong?"

"Nothing is wrong. I walked the pasture we'll use for parking and for the porta-potties. Walked along the creek bed in the back, too. The ground is really good now but if we have rain close to the day, cars will be stuck. I just know it."

"Harry, we've been over this. The Boy Scouts are in charge of parking. Actually, they aren't called Boy Scouts anymore, but you know what I mean. Their parents will be here and we have ten . . . count them, ten . . . fathers who are bringing their dually trucks, complete with heavy chains. If anyone is stuck, they'll be pulled out plus fathers know how to push."

"I know, I know," came the weak reply.

"Stop worrying. The scouts get the parking money, and they'll do very well. For God's sake, don't bring it up. That was one of our biggest fights with the county commissioners. We were showing favoritism."

"That was dreary. They wanted to do it. No other group stepped forward. If anyone was the least bit perverse, the quilting circle could have demanded the job. I would have paid to see that."

"Me too, but the quilters are way too smart. And don't forget, they get a booth in the gym. We have fifteen booths now, which will endear our project to many. Hey, everyone wins. Our history will be preserved. Infuriating as Plecker's laws were, we need to remember. Especially our kids. And bad as that was, look how many successful people the school turned out.

"Which reminds me, Ned says the panels with the names of all graduates painted on them will be ready to be picked up this Wednesday. They've been weatherproofed. Finding a sign painter in Richmond, he got such a big discount. We really had to take that price. I still wish we could have done this on brass plaques, but that would have cost a fortune. We'll have them lining the walls of the gym. If we could have afforded brass, though, we could have put them on the outside of the buildings."

"We'd be in hock for a decade. But it will be nice in the gym. When school classes come through in the fall and winter, they will be impressed to see the names. This place is going to be busy." Harry felt positive about that.

"Seems like a miracle, doesn't it?"

"I don't think I'll believe it until the day is over. Oh, almost forgot, I found an old belt buckle, it's been squashed a bit. It looks like a Union soldier's buckle. We didn't have any skirmishes back there, though."

"Give it to Sherry Evenfall. She knows that stuff. Look how many years she taught History." Then Susan added, "And remember Miranda Hogendobber will be putting plants in front of the schools' windows. She'll wait until we're close to the big day for that."

"Good idea. Okay, I had my moment. Need to take the crew home."

As they squeezed into the 1978 Ford half-ton, Mrs. Murphy on Harry's lap, Pewter behind her on the bench seat, with Pirate and Tucker on the front passenger seat, they marveled at the dogwoods finally opening. Redbuds came early this year, dogwoods opened late.

"I hope this turns out." Harry petted Mrs. Murphy.

"*We all do,*" the animals replied.

4

May 7, 2024

Tuesday

Lucas pitched hay bales onto the back of a flatbed hooked up to Aunt Tally's dually truck. He then hopped up and arranged them in rows. When the rows grew high, he took two long straps, tied them over the bales. Haying filled the air with marvelous scent—clean, fresh—you could almost smell the calories. Then he crawled into the cab, fired up the motor with the pleasing low reverberation. Slowly he drove down the well-maintained farm road to the hay barn; carefully he backed up, cut the motor, and then got out. Unhooking the straps and stacking the hay in the barn took another hour. The sun was fading. He'd have to finish the east field tomorrow.

Not being born a farm boy, Lucas applied himself to learning the chores, the haying, weedwacking and fence lines, throwing out the poorer-quality hay for the cattle, saving the rich stuff for the horses.

He'd come to central Virginia at the end of the bitter winter. Bitter in all respects, for Lucas's job as a secretary to a Republican delegate in the General Assembly ended through no fault of his own. He'd been hit by a car, had to recover. His boss lost her office. Ned Tucker had taken a liking to him, as had Susan and Harry. Richmond accentuated his despondency. He visited the Tuckers, staying in their guesthouse. Once he felt he might make a go of it in the community, he started looking for places to live. This is never easy, no matter where one finds oneself. With everyone's help, he wound up living in a small clapboard farmhouse built for workers on Aunt Tally's lovely estate. At 103, she could no longer do chores. Her great-niece and husband traveled so much, as they bred Thoroughbreds. Finding anyone who knew farmwork or wanted to do it proved a steep problem. Harry and Susan took the fellow—not tall, average height, good shape—to meet the old, bright lady. They charmed each other. He was quite honest about his ignorance but said he wanted to learn. Perfect for Aunt Tally, as she could teach someone plus talk about the old days.

Having finished stacking hay in the well-built hay barn—all the structures on the old estate had been built to last and they did—he left the flatbed and truck where they were, as he'd be at it again in the morning. That hay needed to get up, as rain was forecast for Thursday. All the hayfields had been cut, the lines turned, hay dried. Only fifteen acres remained, but that was a lot for one man to do. The hay cutters did their job, but did not put the stuff up, as they were on to another cutting. Given the unreliability of late-spring weather, you had a narrow window of time to cut those grass crops before they went to seed, much nutrition going with them.

Dusting himself off, Lucas knocked at Aunt Tally's back door. Teresa Becker, the live-in nurse, called to come in. Aunt Tally's dachshund, Bitsy, rushed to greet him. Teresa peeked at the back-porch door.

"Lucas, come on in. She's having a glass of sherry."

Lucas, early forties, followed Teresa and Bitsy to the living room, sunset light bathing the room with soft color.

"Hello. Sit down." The old lady pointed to the chair.

"Oh, that feels good."

"I'll have Teresa take me out tomorrow. Love the smell of fresh-cut hay."

"Me too," he agreed.

"Teresa, bring Lucas some refreshment. Sherry? Whiskey? I have some good rye. I know few people drink it anymore. Too bad. You look like you need a pick-me-up."

"Thank you. Yes, I do need a pick-me-up. This is a bit pedestrian, but I would like anything cold. Co-Cola, iced tea, water with ice cubes."

"Beer?" She was hoping he would take a drink with her.

"Perfect." He beamed.

As the light slowly dimmed, Teresa turned on the lamps, the bottoms being Chinese jars.

"You have a good hay crop. Harry said she has one, too." Lucas took a refreshing sip.

"Never tire of hay or my small peach orchard. Well, how is it going for the big opening day?"

"I think it's good. My job will be getting the old fence line cleaned up. As you know, it's Tazio's and the gang's hard work. I came on board at the end. What dedication they have."

"Yes. As you know, Susan's grandfather was our governor. She was born knowing how to get things done. Harry's mother was the librarian, her father farmed. Her husband, have you ever seen a man that tall and muscular? Fair could lift my house off its foundation." She laughed. "But the committee is full of people who can handle everything."

"Am I still your date?" He smiled at her.

"You and Teresa. I so want to see this dedication. I remember the school, you know. Of course, I didn't go there but I knew many who did. In fact, I heard Tinsley Barton will attend. She's ten years younger than I am. Crozet, Albemarle County, there was a time when we all knew one another." She paused. "That's probably true everywhere."

"Yes, I think so, too."

Shifting in her seat, feet on a big hassock, Aunt Tally looked out the window. "Have you ever noticed how twilight lingers around the spring equinox then slowly grows shorter as we move into summer?"

"A little bit. I spent too much time behind my desk, so my idea of going out was to the gym."

"Being a secretary to any elected official is punishing. Susan's husband needs more help. Susan does some things for him, but a delegate or a state senator needs someone in their district who can travel or spend time in Richmond during the session."

"It's true. There's a reason mostly people with money run for office, and it's difficult for them, too. Another world."

"Indeed. Do you ever miss it?"

"No. I thought I would. I wanted to be useful, but Aunt Tally, it's so wasteful. Party politics is a curse."

She laughed. "General Washington warned us. Well, no matter. I've seen a few great leaders, many good ones, and some real stinkers. In time they're forgotten. Who remembers Garfield? Had he not been assassinated, he would have been a good president, I think; but then, I like history. I'll go off on a toot. Back to you. Harry tells me you might be looking for a house. Stay here, Lucas. Put your money away. There is no need to leave unless you don't like it."

"I love it. I love working outside. I've learned so much, and I'm building muscle." He grinned.

"Never hurts a fellow to have big biceps." She smiled. "Perhaps the house is too small. Was for workers, as you know."

"Perfect size. The fireplace in the kitchen and the one in the living room make it homey. I'm not one for modern architecture."

"Well, this surely isn't modern; 1824. Tell me why you are looking for a home."

"Your niece and her husband are on the road with their daughter. They may not like me when they get back. Even if they do like me, they might like the place not to have anyone else living in it."

"They'll be fine. Your work helps them, too. Blair can do farmwork but he is now part of her business, so his labor here is erratic. He was a model, you know."

"I heard that."

Aunt Tally laughed. "So many people thought he was gay. Too pretty. Well, when he courted and married Little Mim, some said it was for her money. Over time, most people have realized it is a love match. As you know, Big Mim is my niece, Little Mim is really my great-niece. Little Mim and Big Mim don't always get along. Anyway I mean it, stay here. Save your money. If the time comes when you want a bigger house or one you own, you'll be in better shape."

"You don't think my being trans will upset them?"

"No. People can be or say whatever they want. It's what you do that counts. You are a hard worker. I wasn't sure if a political secretary could manage farmwork. Takes so much energy."

"You are kind to think about me."

"I'm old. Ancient really. I like being around younger people. I like thinking I can be helpful. All that old lady wisdom, you know." She laughed.

"You don't seem old. You're so interested in what's going on, have so much vitality."

"You know, Lucas, there are people who die at thirty but we don't bury them until they're eighty. I vowed never to be one of them. Now, tell me, have you met any interesting young people?"

"I'm not young. Nearing fifty."

"Fifty is nothing." She pointed at him. "You've only now got sense to come in out of the rain. Oh, while I'm thinking of weather, you might want a fire in your fireplace tonight. It's going to sink back to the forties but will warm up to the mid-sixties tomorrow. This has been an odd spring. Of course, you can turn up the heat. I much prefer a fire. Now, I'm told that's polluting. So it may be, but it's certainly cheaper than electricity. Nothing smells like a crackling fire." She paused. "Yes, I have pots of money, but I hate to waste it."

He nodded. "My mother is the same way. She doesn't have pots, but she is careful. Anything can happen."

"Well, yes. I try not to focus on money. The men returning from the war, World War II, left such an impression on me. There weren't enough jobs, you see. Soldiers wore their uniforms with the insignia taken off. Many lived in the Quonset huts built during the war for storage. And then, as you know, women who had been in the workforce were pushed back into the home. Some wanted to return, but others didn't. A stressful time. I often think the time after a war is more interesting than the war itself. There's social change, emotional, how shall I say it, repression? No one truly wants to remember whatever happened during the war. Anyway, seeing the problems was the first time I thought about money. We girls weren't taught anything about money. Big Mim's mother was my sister, you see. She married well. I didn't marry at all. Oh, Lucas, I simply couldn't marry some fatuous rich toad. I'm being mean, but that's what was pushed at me. And I fell in love with Harry's grandfather. He hadn't a sou. My family adamantly opposed the match. I wasn't strong enough to resist. He told me he didn't want to ruin my life. So the relationship was severed by both families." A long pause followed this. "Whenever I see Harry I see some of her grandfather in her. Well, I'm nattering on. A vice of old age, I fear. But you'll meet people. Put yourself out there. You're a good-looking fellow."

Lucas blushed. "Thank you. At some point my being trans comes up. Some women reject me right off the bat. I'm a bit shy."

"Nonsense. A girl is lucky to have you. You put yourself out there." She leaned forward. "Lucas, don't be a coward. I was a coward. Here I sit at 103 and I think of Larry every day of my life. I should have fought back. We could have run off. So what if we would be poor as church mice? Yes, I was raised rich, but so what? What else is there but love?"

Lucas, seeing her emotion, got up, walked over to her, picked up her hand, and kissed it. "Aunt Tally, thank you. I guess I don't believe in myself, don't believe a woman would want me. You have helped me. I'll try. And if you can tolerate it, I'll come for more advice." He kissed her hand again.

"Dear boy, you can ask me anything. First piece of advice: When we go to the schools celebration, don't get fussed up. Most people will be in casual clothes, many in jeans. But you be sure to wear a shirt that shows off your arms, roll the sleeves, show your forearms. Your biceps will fill the sleeves. Women like strong arms and you're getting them. Farmwork does it every time." She grinned.

"I'll do just that. And I promise I won't date any woman seriously until you look her over." He kissed her on the cheek.

As he left, stepping out into the night, which was turning cold, he was oddly elated, and ran all the way to his house.

5

May 8, 2024

Wednesday

Magnifying glass in hand, Sherry bent over the damaged buckle, which she had laid on a white towel on the desk surface. "See." Harry took the glass from her hands, squinting one eye. "Rust. Like old cuts, bent on the right side a little. Is it authentic?"

"Oh yes." Sherry pulled a book over on the desk, slipping it open to a page marked by a paper clip. "Look here."

"Second Massachusetts Regiment Infantry. Well, don't these buckles all look alike?"

"Size varies. Some have the regiment marked on the reverse side. Buttons identified a soldier more than a belt buckle. The insignia on his uniform identified his rank, as you know. But this is a Union buckle from the war."

"Mrs. Evenfall, what's it doing at the school?"

"Harry, will you please stop calling me Mrs. Evenfall. We're long past that."

"Yes, ma'am. It's hard when you've known someone from childhood. That person is always your superior."

"Well, I don't know about that, but yes, I do understand the remnants of the titles. Anyway, you know there always have been rumors of a prisoner-of-war camp. We have ample evidence for the one at Barracks Road for the British captives . . . Hessians too . . . during the Revolutionary War. Nothing has ever been found for the war of 1861–1865. I cite the dates because the war may have ended in 1865, but much lingered. The South was occupied. Some of my people fled to wherever the trains carried them. Some of us stayed here." She smiled weakly. "Better the devil you know than the devil you don't."

Harry smiled. "Makes sense to me." She paused. "But, Sherry, if there was a camp for prisoners of war, why aren't there pieces of it left or markers in the ground? You know, filled-in postholes, stuff like that. Look what's happening in York, Pennsylvania. The historical group in York has finally found the place where a building stood. The postholes, after careful searching, examining photographs for a couple of years, were finally identified. They found other things, but this put the icing on the cake. Granted, it was the Revolutionary War, but you'd think it would be easier for us to find such evidence, as the Civil War is closer in time."

Sherry touched the buckle. "People don't like to focus on prisoners of war. You wouldn't mind if I cleaned this up, would you?"

"Of course not. Keep it."

"Finders, keepers." Sherry smiled. "Here's what I suspect happened. The South lacked the funds to build decent dwellings. Maybe all they had were tents or makeshift shelters made from pine logs, needles, leaves, and such stuffed between the logs to try to keep out the weather. I am willing to bet they did what they could . . . cut logs, created lumber for some kind of floor. Raised floors help in the rain and snow. But if it was only a tent, one could cut a hole through it, surround it with something nonflammable, slide a pipe through it, get a stove to sit on slate, of which we have a fair amount around here, then at least men could be kept warm in the winter. If there wasn't a stove, they could build a chimney from charred logs. Certainly there was enough wood for firewood. When the war ended, it would have been easy to take down the tents and break up the floors, so I don't think there would be evidence. And you know those prisoners hurried home as soon as they could. Given that buildings were destroyed here, all over, women and children may have used those tents until their husbands returned, if indeed they survived. We can't imagine the suffering of women and children, whatever their status."

"Going on today." Harry sighed.

"It will never end. My studies of history force me to say that with great conviction." Sherry picked up the buckle. "I wonder if whoever wore this died or lived? Maybe he was so sick of the war, he threw it away."

"I'd think if prisoners died, we'd know where they were buried. We have a rough idea at the Barracks. What a pity that the camp was allowed to disintegrate."

"Most people don't wish to keep their prisons. As a war drags on, it becomes harder and harder to feed prisoners, much less your own men. You do know the British treated our prisoners as traitors. So many of our captured died. And we weren't a country yet, so every state had their own ideas. How Washington persevered, I will never know. Those signing up for their state militia at times didn't have to serve a full year. They could leave when their time was up, and did. The Constitutional Congress couldn't get states to pay their bills, to send more men. Granted, the solution was quite different than during the Civil War, but if the troops struggled to eat so did the prisoners."

Harry, mind racing, said, "If we ever found evidence of a prisoner-of-war camp, it might protect the school forever."

"What do you mean?"

"I worry a real estate developer would tear down those buildings after all the work we've done to restore the schools. But when the day comes that Jim Sanburne is no longer our mayor, who is to say what will happen? That nice land in the back will make a pretty development at enormous profit for a developer and the city would make money twice: First with the sale, second with the taxes when the houses are sold, lived in. Lots of money. Jim has protected us."

Sherry's face registered this. "What a terrible thought."

"I'd like to see a park or two. There's no place to publicly congregate."

"Let's not make public your find. I'd like to do more research."

"Of course. You'd think there might be a mention in family records."

"Maybe. But so much was destroyed after the war. Especially service records. People like Senator Thaddeus Stevens wanted Confederate soldiers to be tried as traitors." She sighed. "The desire for revenge does nothing but create more revenge as soon as the defeated or their children have recovered enough to bring sorrows on the victors. If there was some sort of camp here, it is more than possible that anyone connected to it would've been endangered. Fortunately, that didn't happen. As it was, it was bad enough."

"Yes." Harry stared at the belt buckle again. "Wasn't much to Crozet then."

Sherry laughed. "There isn't much to Crozet today. Well, more housing developments. It's small, quiet, not given to distinguished architecture."

"Mirador." Harry named the estate famous for producing four gorgeous daughters, one of whom became Lady Astor.

"Simple but lovely. People out here farmed, built solid homes, sturdy outbuildings."

"Stables sometimes were lovelier than the homes. Well, I'm not an Architecture History major, but I enjoy visiting homes, especially during garden week. Makes me jealous," Harry confessed. "I envy those beautiful gardens. I don't have time to create anything like that, nor do I have the help."

"I've seen your climbing roses, your peonies, pansies everywhere."

"Oh, Sherry, you flatter me. You go to the big estates or places with famous landscape architects, the gardens' colors alone will knock you out. Mother loved climbing roses, the old-fashioned tea roses, too. I've kept her plants going."

"She had an eye." Sherry smiled, remembering the long-departed woman.

Harry noticed an open crossword puzzle book. "Since when have you tackled crossword puzzles?"

"Mmm, it's more Moz than me, but when he loses his temper over one, I see if I can figure it out. Look here." She pointed to a puzzle, a fairly simple one. "The clues can be confusing. He thought 'green as the sea.' I thought 'green as a lea.' Turns out I was right. He finished the puzzle and left in a good mood."

As Harry drove home, she thought about how chaotic it must have been in the late 1800s. Fields needed to be brought back to productivity. New wells needed to be dug. The victors usually befouled the wells. Most all of the horses had been stolen or taken by either side. Same with the mules. Little by little, those men and women determined to live in Virginia found cattle, grew hay, managed to buy a horse or mule, thanks to a decent crop of corn or vegetables. Times were difficult even for the rich, but for an average farmer it had to be hell.

The soft breeze, cool, slipped through her opened truck window. She closed it. Sherry knew so much. Loved research, never tired of applying herself to what had been brushed aside. Harry would not have thought of the destroyed records, the fear, but Sherry did. No wonder she had been a beloved teacher and now a stalwart of the Historical Society.

Once home, the first thing she did was build a fire in the library.

"*That will feel good.*" Mrs. Murphy watched how carefully Harry built a fire.

"*It's getting cold.*" Pewter lounged on the sofa before the fire. "*She keeps the electricity on, set low, but she's not going to risk pipes.*"

"*Boy, that would be an expensive mess,*" Tucker, who had carried a piece of kindling to Harry, agreed.

"*It's supposed to be freezing again tonight.*" Mrs. Murphy listened to the weather forecast on TV, one of the few things Harry watched.

"*The changing seasons fool you. Here it is, early May, and people have to bring in their plants. Fortunately, most of what we have here is tough. She won't put out potted plants until June.*" Tucker liked helping with the plants.

The corgi would dig a hole if Harry was going to put a new plant in the soil. Tucker couldn't dig out the big pots, which irritated her, as she loved the smell of that good potting soil.

Fire finally leaping up, the warmth comforting, Harry sat on the sofa next to her cats while Tucker and Pirate sprawled in front of the fire.

She sat there spellbound by the flames.

"I have an idea," she addressed her friends. "I'll buy a drone. Well, I'll get Fair to buy a drone. And I'll take pictures of the land behind the school. Who's to say? Something might show up."

6

May 9, 2024

Thursday

Drizzle slid down the back of Harry's neck. Her Barbour coat, twenty-plus years old, kept the rain out as good as the day she bought it. But nothing really could keep rain off one's neck or from sneaking into the back of one's boots. Next to her, Lucas, in a new mid-thigh Wilson raincoat, had wrapped a scarf around his neck. Smart. Kept his neck somewhat dry.

The two stood at the stream at the western part of Aunt Tally's farm. This stream traversed Reverend Jones's property, then Harry's. All waters eventually poured into the Chesapeake Bay.

This creek, named for whatever properties it passed through in the late eighteenth century, also flowed past the schools, along Crozet, thence through Albemarle County. Aunt Tally called it Swift Creek.

Tucker and Pirate stood with the humans. Although Pirate's double coat, thicker and longer than Tucker's, repelled rain, both dogs had wet outer coats.

The cats had stayed home. While it wasn't hot, only low sixties, Harry didn't want to keep them in the truck with the windows closed, nor did she have any desire to sit on a soaked seat. Even if just cracked, the opening meant the seat would get wet. If the wind blew sideways, they'd get soaked.

The drone, which Fair purchased yesterday evening for Harry, sat at their feet. Eastward, the waters widened, picking up speed. Fast moving, the creek could fool you. If you stepped in, you'd be swept off your feet. Here and there, deep holes existed, but you couldn't see them until you stepped in one. Like any water, standing like a lake or flowing as a hard-running creek, you could never truly trust it.

Peering, eyes squinting, Harry said, "I can't see any obstruction."

"I can't either, but her easternmost meadow, the one abutting the old Jones place, has had standing water . . . mmm, maybe two or three inches after every rain. So I thought if I could see the water during the rain, I might find the source. As you know, it flows west to east," Lucas said.

"You walked the creek bed?"

He nodded. "I did, which is why I'm determined to figure this out. Looking into the water from the creek bed, I couldn't see anything. Again, I was on this side, since the other side is more difficult."

"Is," Harry agreed. "The only time it gets muddy is after a biblical rain."

"Thanks for bringing the drone over. Susan told me you just got it."

"The town crier." Harry laughed.

He laughed, too. "She is at the center of everything. The Tuckers have been so good to me, as have you and Fair."

"Glad you moved?"

"I am. Love Aunt Tally."

"She can use some spirited chat. Teresa is not known for her conversational abilities, but she's a terrific nurse. Big Mim found her, and she's a relief to us all. Aunt Tally is amazing. She rode until she was ninety-eight. Granted, she was walking, not trotting or galloping, but there she was. Rode her bicycle, too. Then she began to lose her balance a bit. She protested, but finally realized age was limiting her. I'm thrilled you're in the Rose Cottage. Now that it's returned to life, you can replant the climbing roses."

"You'll have to help me. I know nothing about plants. But I do know if we don't send this thing up, we are going to get caught in harder rain. The clouds are dipping lower." He pointed to the sky.

"Right." She bent over, picking up the drone, handing it to him. "It's not heavy." She wiped off the camera with her handkerchief, returning it to her pocket.

He placed the drone back on the ground. "I'm ready."

She handed him the camera as she punched the on button then guided the drone up, not too high. When the buzz receded from their hearing, Lucas peered at the screen while Harry half looked at it, guiding the drone.

"Higher? Lower?"

"You got it about right." He grumbled, "Not even a sunken branch."

"There's more to go. I'll send this down to Cooper's, then back up on the other side of the creek."

Cynthia Cooper, a deputy in the sheriff's department, had bought the Jones place, which abutted both Harry's and Aunt Tally's farm.

Pirate sat quietly, while Tucker leaned on Harry. She could have easily wedged under the truck, but she didn't mind the rain. Tucker's job was to stick close to Harry. Pirate felt the same. Humans missed so much.

"Nothing." Lucas was disappointed.

"Okay, coming back on the western side of the creek. I'll fly close to the bank unless there's an obstacle. You'd think there'd be more downed trees."

"Aunt Tally says she keeps the farm open back there, or used to do so. Hardly anyone left to work here, but it seems Blair keeps things up when he's around."

"When he is, he fixes the roads, clears branches fallen on them, repairs fences, but he's gone half the year now. Aunt Tally worked outside into her mid-eighties. Can't find people willing to work outside anymore."

"No one knows farmwork, and that includes me. I'm learning." He kept his eye on the screen. "Stop the drone a minute. Look."

She, beeper in hand, peered intently. "Don't remember that. Whatever it is, it's under the water. Let me see if this thing can get lower."

"Looks like a car bumper." Lucas then tilted his head. "How could people have missed that? I mean, over the years."

Harry took the drone screen from his hand. "It does look like a car bumper. It's possible, if it is a car, that it wasn't here. We've had terrific storms these past few years. Could have washed down from upstream. Parts of this creek are wide. Well, let's look."

"I don't know if you can drive all the way there. Much of the old farm road on that side has some huge potholes. Aunt Tally has mentioned it a few times. I've been busy on this side of the creek, near the house and the farm buildings, so I haven't investigated."

"Well, now's the time. Come on. You'll have two wet dogs for companions."

"Won't feel a thing. What I like about this coat is that it's not stiff. I can move in it and I have a sherpa lining I can put in during the winter."

"That was smart. I have too many coats."

"Susan says you can't throw anything out."

"Well," a pause, "what if I need something but I threw it out in a cleaning fit? But clothes weren't as versatile when I bought coats. I should go through everything and go to Goodwill with stuff."

Tucker sat on Harry's lap as she drove, while Pirate sat between Lucas and Harry. The old truck had a bench seat, so the huge dog could do it.

The truck rumbled across a sturdy old bridge to the other side of the creek.

"He's such a good boy." Lucas didn't mind the big animal wedged next to him.

"They're very faithful and quiet. I could have put him in Tally's barn, closed the stall door. Didn't occur to me we'd all be in the truck."

"No," Pirate disagreed with a soft voice.

"Good boy." She reached over to pat his head, returning her hand to the wheel, as she had to circumnavigate a nasty pothole.

"This is it," Lucas noted as the road, churned to bits over time, was both unreliable and too narrow. Some of it had fallen into the creek over the decades.

Harry stopped. "We can walk it. Can't be that far."

The four wiggled out of the truck, Tucker being lifted out.

Harry closed the door, Lucas, too. They started heading east.

"Boy, look at all the blackberry bushes. They should be blooming in a week. We're behind this year, thanks to that wicked cold spell we had in February and March."

"I learned to build fires." Lucas smiled.

They trudged on, the rain picking up, mud adhering to their boots.

"There's the poplar on the other side. I go by the trees, any kind of marker." Harry slowed. "We're close."

They walked forty muddy yards then stopped.

Lucas noticed what was a back bumper. "There it is."

"What in the hell is an old car doing here? Well, could have washed up anywhere, I guess, depending on the force of the water."

Lucas leaned over the creek bank. "Can't see anything."

"We'd need bright lights." She also leaned over. "We should call Coop."

Back at Lucas's house, Harry called her neighbor and friend on her cellphone, giving the deputy all the details.

"Could you see the car? Get an idea about its age?"

"No. It's in one of those Swift Creek sinkholes, plus it started to rain hard. Couldn't see much but the bumper, and we only saw that because it was brighter."

"I'll check if we can pull it out. You know the department has to do that, in case of foul play, contraband in the truck. Unlikely, but must be done."

"Okay. Lucas and I will tell Aunt Tally. You can call her when you all are coming over."

"Okay."

After that call, Harry and Lucas sat there in the small, cozy kitchen, hoping to dry out.

"I'll tell Aunt Tally." He looked at the clock. "I'll wait until sherry time."

"You've got an hour." Harry smiled.

"There's a little chill, thanks to the rain. Coffee? Tea?"

"I'll have tea. Let me go to the truck to get bones for those two."

"I have some. I've learned to stock lots for Bitsy."

"That dachshund can eat." Harry smiled as Lucas opened a cabinet, bringing out two fake, juicy bones.

"I like him." Pirate tasted the bone brushed with beef juice.

"Crunchies are the best, but this is good." Tucker gnawed at the treat.

"This is restorative." Harry gratefully took her cup of dark tea. "What is this?"

"Simple Earl Grey."

"Tastes so fresh."

"When I lived in Richmond, there was the best tea store on Cary Street. I got spoiled." He took a sip. "It is good. Feels great to have something warm inside."

"Does. I try to keep a thermos full of hot tea in the truck during the winter when I'm on my rounds. Summer, I keep Perrier with ice cubes in the thermos."

"I don't know which is worse, bitter cold or punishing heat and humidity."

"One thing about farmwork, you just deal with it." She smiled. "I can't understand why people don't want to work outside, anymore. I think you'll live longer working outside barring accidents. You're constantly using your body. Look how long Aunt Tally has lasted. She was outside far more than inside."

"I've grown very fond of her." He allowed his eyelids to droop a tiny bit as he relaxed, the tea adding to his pleasure. "You know, she has never once asked me about being trans. Not once."

"It's not her nature to pry. She was raised a certain way in a certain time. She, Big Mim, they both have impeccable manners."

"I can see that. My mother and father don't have fancy manners. I'd describe them as severely repressed." He smiled. "They know the basic rules. Thank you, please, excuse me. I fear even those are going by the wayside."

"I wonder. You and I are about the same age." She held up her cup. "So we aren't young. Now we have generations behind us. You notice things. You become more critical."

"It creeps up on you. Working in the State House I learned old Virginia manners. Survival." He grinned.

"That's the truth. I sometimes think good manners are a way to put people in their place in a regulated way. Sometimes people don't even know until hours or days later. I mean, if they haven't been raised in the Virginia way."

"I was raised in Georgia through grade school, came up here for junior and high school, then William and Mary. I realized in junior high there is a Virginia way. Then again, Amanda drilled it into me when we were in the sorority together."

"I bet she did." Harry raised her eyebrows, for Amanda, first a newscaster then a delegate, had been Lucas's friend and boss.

"I was and remain grateful. Harry, every now and then she calls. I haven't the heart to cut her off, but I don't want to see her. Maybe I will someday. I know I'm supposed to forgive, but I'm not there yet."

"She betrayed you on a lot of levels. If you feel like it, talk to Reverend Jones. He has a magical way of helping you see things. He's a wonderful pastor."

"Thank you for the suggestion. I have a lot to learn."

"Don't we all?" She smiled slightly. "Okay, time to feed the horses. I keep their stall doors to the outside open so they can come and go. Sometimes they like the rain. Other times I'll go home and everyone will be in his or her stall."

He stood to walk her to the door. "Thanks for the use of the drone."

"Sure. It was a good test. I wanted a drone so I could check the back acres at the schools before the 'do.' It's a lot to walk, but with the drone I can get a quick look. I'll then walk it. Won't waste time. This should do it. Look what we found."

"Treasure." Lucas laughed.

"Wouldn't it be nice." She kissed him on the cheek, then raced through the raindrops, followed by Tucker and Pirate, to the truck.

Driving home, she thought how odd it was that they'd found a car in the water.

7

May 10, 2024

Friday

The rain continued, making the big tow truck grind up what was left of the farm road. Lucas rose early, cleared a wider path with a machete, and also created a circle using the biggest farm tractor. Deep as the mud could be, those huge tires churned through it. He left the big tractor on the other side of the creek in case it was needed.

Cooper and three officers, one running the big hitch, stood on the bank, as did Harry and the dogs. The youngest officer dove into the water, face mask on, hitching the big metal hook around the bumper. He crawled out, lifted his mask up. While it wasn't a hot day, it wasn't too warm so the water was cold.

Little by little, the tow truck pulled up a 2001 Subaru.

"Good Lord," Lucas exclaimed.

Cooper, saying nothing, continued to direct the tow-truck driver with her hands. Once the car was solidly on the ground, she and the other officers walked over. Harry, Lucas, and the dogs kept their distance.

Hands in surgeon gloves, Cooper opened the driver's door, and water gushed out. A skeleton, still clothed, sat behind the wheel.

Cooper called the sherriff on her cellphone. "Rick, need a team out here. We've got a corpse. Bones. Just got the old car out of the water." She listened. "Okay." She clicked off her phone. "You two go back to Lucas's house. If I need you, I'll come get you. Obviously, don't say anything to Aunt Tally. Rick should do that."

The sheriff, Rick Shaw, would be able to transmit this unwelcome fact to the old lady as gently as possible.

Harry, Lucas, and the dogs sloshed back to the big tractor. Lucas crawled up to sit in the wet seat. Harry followed the machine from a distance. No point having mud flying off the big hind wheels splatter all over her.

Lucas parked the tractor in the large equipment shed, another building that had stood the test of time. Once out, he walked silently with Harry back to his house.

They hung their coats on hooks in the mudroom.

"If you want to peel off your pants, I can go into the living room," Harry offered.

"Good idea. I'll drip everywhere."

Tucker, Pirate, and Harry, wet, sat on the old church bench against the wall. They heard Lucas pad by in the hall. About ten minutes later he joined them, wearing sweatpants.

"Warmer. It's hard to pull off jeans when you're wet. I'm better now."

"Yeah."

They sat there for a moment then Lucas exhaled. "I've never seen a skeleton. Fake ones, but you know."

"I do. It's a shock. Bones. Whoever that was had to have been dead a long time. Think it was a man, because of the clothing. Remarkable how some stuff lasts. I mean, archaeologists open tombs from the Middle Ages in Europe, and the skeletons are wearing their rich finery. Creepy in a way."

"Sure is." He crossed one leg over the other. "What do you think Rick and Cooper will do?"

"First they have to inspect the vehicle. The forensic team will check the corpse, then put it on a stretcher to go to the morgue. Chances of fingerprints are nil, but they'll be extra careful not to disturb anything. It's possible they can determine the cause of death. Once back at headquarters, Cooper and Rick will start searching missing persons reports. Granted, I'm not a cop, but since the car is a 2001, I guess I'd start there. Missing persons from 2001 forward. Could have been purchased as a used car." She added, "Someone somewhere had to file a missing persons report."

Someone did. Cooper found it easily enough, as it had been filed in 2006 in Amherst County for Denver Raiselle, a geology professor at Mary Baldwin College, who never showed up for class after December 2, 2006. Age forty-one. Married. Two children.

Rick called the sheriff in Amherst County. He had been sheriff only since 2021. But he would check their files. The man who was sheriff then was now eighty-two, retired. Rick asked, would he mind if the two of them visited the older fellow? As Amherst was forty-five minutes away, he could be there soon if the old sheriff was available. He was. So Rick hopped in his squad car while Cooper, at her desk, kept searching.

Rick tried not to jump the gun, overthink. He dealt with the facts in front of him. But thoughts intruded. He'd been in law enforcement long enough to realize one of two things had happened. Well, maybe one of three.

First, the driver could have been drunk or fallen asleep, veered off the road into the water. Couldn't get out once awake. Or he could have committed suicide by driving into the water. The ways people chose to kill themselves proved highly personal. Lastly, he could have been murdered, put in the car, and pushed into the water.

He hoped forensics could find proof of violence if it had occurred. Bones told the truth. If evidence was there, his team would find it.

The visit to the old sheriff proved to be all Rick had hoped. The old fellow was concise, stuck to the facts, giving an opinion if asked.

Denver lived at the bottom of Bear Mountain, the home of the Monacan Nation. He was Monacan on his mother's side and participated in the tribe's traditions. He lived the life of a college professor. He was well liked. His main study was the slate belt that ran through places like Farmville, a wide belt that was used for hundreds of years for roofing, walkways, even furniture tops. As the South slowly recovered from the war, slate was used in large quantities in Richmond. Those who owned a part of the wide belt managed a decent living. As far as Sheriff Carter knew, Denver'd had no enemies. His wife and two daughters left the area two years after his disappearance. The last the sheriff had heard of the wife, she was living in Billings, Montana. The girls went to college out there.

"I'll track down his wife," Sheriff Larson, portly, in his fifties, said as they drove away from the tidy rancher.

"I can go over to Mary Baldwin. He'll have a file. Might be someone who remembers him," Rick volunteered.

"Cold cases are hard." Sheriff Larson sighed.

"They are, but I take them as a challenge. At least his family will finally know where he is."

"Yes. Makes me think about all the MIAs from our wars." Sheriff Larson stepped out of the vehicle once they were back at his office. "Keep me posted."

"Likewise."

Driving back to Albemarle County, Rick considered law enforcement. Most of the people in it had a strong sense of right and wrong. You see people at their worst. You can also see them at their best. As for seeing what was left of Denver, he sifted through the facts to date. No report of alcoholism, erratic emotions, drugs, major illness. Some diabetes. He hadn't seen medical records, had only Sheriff Carter's recall about questioning Denver's wife, who had been worried he needed his medication. So a seemingly ordinary man, educated, no apparent major vices, attached to his tribal identity, well respected in his career. Disappeared.

Once back, he hadn't even plopped in his office chair when Cooper knocked on the doorjamb.

"Yes."

She put a piece of paper in front of him. He read it.

"A broken rib over his left side and one in the rear. No other damage to the body. The breaks are consistent with the path of the bullet." He glanced up at her. "Murder?"

"Looks like it. Or suicide. You can shoot yourself through the heart."

"This isn't rock solid—yet." He then told her everything he'd learned in Amherst County, repeating himself. "If someone shot a well-liked man, no one saw it coming."

"But did *he* see it coming?" his good deputy replied.

8

May 11, 2024

Saturday

Standing in Cooper's garden, Harry knelt down to touch a sprig of corn breaking the surface.

"If you plant corn every two weeks, you'll have fresh corn into October. Not that any of us knows what the weather will be, but it's worth stretching out your crop. Some, like corn, you can. Others are harder, like asparagus, which is edible every two years. Then you have to remember to plant each year, knowing half of what you're putting into the soil you won't harvest for two years."

Cooper looked at Harry's right knee. "Your knee is soaked."

"I know. I should have thought of that."

"Come on in the house. Can't do anything about your pants, but we can have a hot something. It's not raw, but the chill creeps in. Still feels like rain."

"Does." Harry followed her friend to the house.

"They'll eat," Pewter declared as she watched from the old Jones's graveyard.

"*Let's not run.*" Tucker liked the graveyard, as it was well tended, peaceful, and the rabbits visited frequently.

"*Why not?*" Pirate asked.

"*It's undignified,*" Tucker responded.

Mrs. Murphy lifted her long silken eyebrows. "*Don't listen to that, Pirate. If we meow at the door, our paws a bit wet, we look hungry, Cooper will give us treats. Mom will tell her not to fall for it, but I know for a fact Cooper keeps treats for us.*"

"*Murphy, we know that.*" Pewter moved ahead of the tabby.

"*Yes, but Pirate doesn't. Mom kept him in the truck when she'd come by. He was awkward as a puppy. He knocked stuff over at the house, in the bar. Can't do that to someone else's house.*" Murphy caught up with Pewter, as did Pirate.

"*I'm all grown now.*"

Pewter glanced up at the huge animal. "*Yes, but don't let that give you any ideas. I run things around here.*"

"*No you don't.*" Tucker zoomed ahead of the others, reaching the back door, where she tapped on it with her front paw and let out a loud whimper.

"*She's so full of it,*" Pewter grumbled. "*She has no idea about how much I do. Harry couldn't even wash the dishes without my supervision. I have to sit on the counter and check everything.*"

The others reached the back door. Pewter meowed with vigor and Pirate tapped the door, which sounded like a rap.

Harry opened the door. "Stay right there." She returned in a few moments with an old scarf. She knelt down to wipe off everyone's paws, Cooper came up behind her.

"Harry, I don't care about wet paw prints."

"I do." Finishing her task, Harry folded the dripping red bandanna, setting it on the back step.

"*Act grateful,*" Pewter hissed under her breath to the Irish Wolfhound.

Pirate looked up at Harry and Cooper with his sweetest expression. Pewter brushed against Harry's leg while Mrs. Murphy rubbed on Cooper. Tucker sat, a big smile on her face.

Cooper walked to a cabinet, pulled out cat treats, a bag of dog treats, and gave everyone two treats.

"You're spoiling them." Harry smiled.

"Learned it from you."

The two women returned to the table, where Harry sipped a Co-Cola and Cooper enjoyed port. She loved port no matter the time of day.

It was an ingrained thing to sit with your friends, glass in hand. Even if you stood outside the door, you'd be asked in. If you were dirty your friend would hand you a glass and come out to sit with you. There were always chairs outside.

"That's all we know." Cooper had finished telling Harry what she and Sheriff Shaw had discovered about the skeleton. It was also on the morning's news. Weekends were slow for news, so an unsolved death proved a boon for them.

"You two got to work fast."

"We did. This will hold people's interest for a day or two. Something immediate will happen and the Denver Raiselle situation will fade, unless we miraculously solve an old murder quickly. People here have the attention span of a gnat."

"So this is the proverbial cold case?" Harry inquired.

"It is. In a murder case, the first forty-eight hours are critical. You get the most information. Something like this, eighteen years, there's not much hope, but things do occur . . . someone may remember a fact that leads you to the truth."

"What could a geologist know that would get him killed, if he didn't shoot himself?"

"Anything. An affair gone wrong. Forgery. There's no end to crimes. His profession may have had nothing to do with it."

"Could being Monacan be important?" Harry knew about his affiliation as that was in the news.

"Possibly. Pamunkey tribes finally got recognized July 2, 2015. Took until 2017 for six more tribes to be recognized. I think a few remain unrecognized." Cooper shook her head. "There's a spot in hell for Plecker. You don't realize what damage a public servant can do until faced with it. We concentrate on elected officials. Anyone in government, elected or appointed, can create misery. There's no way to know if Professor Raiselle was quietly involved in trying to get government recognition. It could have created trouble at Mary Baldwin at the time. Then again, not. So many of those people are retired or gone."

Harry laughed. "I guess if given the opportunity, any of us can create havoc."

"More Coke?"

"Cooper, it's Co-Cola."

"Well, where I come from it's Coke. Some parts of the country call it pop. Expressions are funny. After I graduated from college, I was lucky enough to get a summer job in Australia. It was winter there. Anyway, went there, rented a room near the University of Melbourne, and the first night I was there the owner asked when I would like him to knock me up. I sputtered. Then he repeated it, but asked for the time. I was a little dense but I realized he meant when he should knock on my door to wake me."

"Funny. I remember my father asked for a barefoot cup of coffee when we visited Boston. Had to explain that meant no milk." Harry glanced at her animals happily chewing. "You know, they say that animals can understand languages are different, so I guess they hear accents even better than we do." She thought a moment. "It was shocking yesterday realizing there was someone in that old car. Were you surprised?"

"Sure. Just because I'm a cop doesn't mean I am used to something like that. If I walk into a house where there's been a shooting, seeing a corpse doesn't surprise me. Finding bodies that have been hidden, stuff like that, is much more difficult. Even when you're looking for a victim or a missing person, finding them can be a jolt. Seeing a skeleton in the car, yeah, a jolt. When you think of it, Harry, there are so many ways to die."

Truer words were never spoken.

9

May 12, 2024

Sunday

"This is far enough." Susan stopped walking. "No one is going to cause a problem all the way this far behind the schools."

"I don't think so either, but it can't hurt to look over what's here. Old pastures. Time to bush-hog, too. But we know from the old drawings where the creek flowed. That changed. Water changes everywhere. So that's why Fair and I bought this drone. Actually, he bought it."

Harry picked up the drone, not heavy but a bit awkward. "What's unnerving is what this discovered when I used it over at Aunt Tally's. Lucas wanted to check the old farm road, knew I had a new toy, and asked me over."

"All that time in the water. Did the car move from miles away in successive floods or was it near Aunt Tally's farm all that time?" Susan grimaced.

"I doubt we'll know. Pirate, move a bit." Harry petted the dog's head. "If I turn around too fast, I'll bump right into you."

"*Okay.*" The big fellow took a few steps to her right.

"*You don't need a drone. I can see lots,*" Pewter called out from the poplar she'd climbed.

"*If she wanted to, she could climb a tree.*" Mrs. Murphy sat on a branch below Pewter. "*I like climbing the sycamores because the bark peels.*"

"*Me too.*" Pewter observed Susan placing the drone on the ground. "*There she goes.*"

Harry, beeper in hand, sent the drone down the creek. Both women looked at the creek.

"You know what we really need. Old photographs. We have no way to compare."

"You can see where the water has cut the banks deeper," Susan replied.

"Look. There's the X I made out of stones. That's where I found the Union buckle. I told you what Sherry said. Looks the same."

"You did. I doubt we'll find records from that time, records that could compromise someone. Then again, you never know if an old diary is up in the attic of one of our homes from that period. We've got homes from the mid-1700s. Of course, go down to Charles City, down to the Potomac, some of those gorgeous estates were built in the 1600s."

"Don't you think you can tell a lot by the way people lived?"

"Sure. Look at my grandmother's house. Next to Beau Pre. All that stuff back there off Garth Road."

"Now, there's something." Harry stopped the drone.

She was learning how useful a drone could be.

"A golf club?" Susan murmured.

"Did you throw a golf club back there?" Harry teased her.

"I have never thrown a golf club, and you know that. You've caddied for me since high school." Susan stuck her face close to the screen. "That's not an old club."

"Well, someone's been practicing, lost their temper." Harry laughed. "Let's leave it but tell our group and ask if anyone has been driving back there."

"The only person who plays golf besides me in our group is my husband. I've heard Tazio has gotten hooked on pickleball."

"She's too young to play pickleball," Harry replied.

"No. Young people are coming to it. It's fast and easier to learn than tennis. Are you at the end of the property yet?"

"Just about. I use the big hickory as a marker. Okay, coming back."

The drone soon arrived, drifted down. Harry cut the motor and the propellers slowed.

"Realtors love these things." Susan listened as the whirr puttered then stopped.

"You still have to walk the land. If Lucas and I had ignored the shine in the water, we wouldn't have found the car. It looked like a bumper. I could get the drone close, but we still had to walk to it."

"What an awful find. I spoke to Aunt Tally. She seems okay, but she hopes the professor wasn't murdered on her land all those years ago."

"I hope not, too. Well, here's what I see today. People can easily walk in from the back. Not that such a thing involves wrongdoing. I'm more curious about foot traffic now that I found the buckle."

"Maybe it's not important."

Harry reached down to pet Tucker. "People do stupid things. Maybe the buckle was dropped."

"That they do. Don't worry about the buckle."

"You're right. I'm kind of twitchy since finding that body. To change the subject, I've been using this drone on your walnut stand. Driving to the top of those acres is fun, but this way I can check on wildlife, see if anyone has messed with the trees."

As they walked back to the schools, Susan said, "A bit of those walnuts belong to you. I was lucky my uncle gave them to me in his will. It's a safety net, you know. Ned makes a good living, but if anything happened I've got the walnuts."

"You'll inherit the Holloways' estate. Your mother and grandmother will see to that."

"Yes, I will, but I hope not for decades. Grandmother will go eventually. She's strong as a horse, but you never know. Mom, she'd better make it into her eighties." Susan took a deep breath. "Funny, the older I get, the more I rely on my mother's wisdom. I certainly didn't when young."

Harry reached over, putting her hand on Pirate's back, as the wolfhound was sticking right with her. "Think that's true of everyone."

"Whee." Mrs. Murphy skidded backwards down the tree.

"Here I come." Pewter carefully backed down. *"I like climbing up better than coming down."*

The two cats raced toward the buildings, flashing past the humans and the dogs.

"Show-off," Tucker grumbled. *"She can't help herself."*

"Pretty good for a fat cat." Pirate's voice carried.

Pewter stopped in her tracks, turned. *"I am not fat."*

"Don't reply," Tucker advised. *"This will go on and on."*

Pirate followed Tucker's advice.

Pewter held her head high as she walked with deliberation toward the high school building.

Susan unlocked the school's back door. Harry, carrying the drone, stepped in, as did the animals. The women walked to two desks and sat down, getting their breath after the walk. Harry placed the drone on the floor.

The uneven pine floors gave the interior an almost colonial look. The plain walls, some framed photographs, led a student's eyes to the teacher's desk on the dais. One would need to twist around to stare out the long windows. No doubt, many a student did, lost in a daydream until the teacher broke the spell.

Harry so often felt a part of these surroundings. Sitting in a classroom involved boredom, wanting to be outside, shutting out your teacher's voice if only for a moment, all feelings students had experienced since Plato's school in ancient Athens. No matter how good the teacher, sometimes one's mind wasn't there.

"Sweater weather." Susan stared at the stove, adding, "Still chilly. If we were going to work in here, I'd put logs in the stove. Sometimes I think a chill gets to you faster than genuine cold. But midday or late afternoon, it's T-shirt weather.

"Say, did I tell you what's going on at the State House?"

"No. I hope everyone received invitations to our dedication."

"Ned said they did. I think a few delegates and senators might drive over. Here's what's going on: Virginia is addressing the need for doctors in rural and underserved areas. Well, Kathy Tran, head of the Democratic Caucus in the House of Delegates, sponsored a bill to reduce doctor shortages by making it easier for immigrant doctors to be certified. Think of that."

"That's solid progress." Harry was surprised. "What's more impressive, that both Democrats and Republicans are cooperating, or that government is planning for a potential crisis? I've kind of given up, you know."

She thought a moment. She recalled Lucas's former boss. "You and I have to give Amanda Fields credit. For all the fighting she stirred up in the House, she did get women from both parties cooperating."

"She's out of jail, isn't she? Ned said something to that effect. Got off for good behavior. Does Lucas ever mention her?"

"Not much."

"I can understand that. She hung him out to dry. Oh, we got off track. Back to doctors. We have good doctors in Virginia, are in a well-served area. Ned says the drive behind pushing for more doctors is that everyone should be able to see a doctor when they need one." She added, "You know we have fabulous pathologists, too."

Harry grinned. "Why do we have such good pathologists?"

Susan laughed. "Hey, we're good to our dead."

"Someone wasn't good to Denver Raiselle. This wouldn't bother me so much if I hadn't seen his bones. There are lots of unsolved murders. Seeing one is another matter."

"Yes." Susan turned to see Mrs. Murphy chase a little mouse,

which scurried back into its barely visible hole in the teacher's desk leg. "What a little stinker."

"Mice are in all the buildings, but not in huge numbers. Susan, there's no way to keep out mice, even with cats."

"Bet a Jack Russell could do it." Susan mentioned a ferocious ratter.

"Worthless," Tucker barked. *"Impossible. I can do much better."*

"They do catch mice and rats. More than you do, Bubblebutt." Pewter flicked her tail.

Tucker lunged for Pewter. The race was on.

"All right. Susan, let's go. They'll make a mess, God knows what they'll knock over, and we'll have to deep clean everything again.

"Out! Out!" Harry opened the front door as Susan locked the back one.

Pewter shot out the front door, climbed right up a sugar maple as Tucker barked below.

Harry walked back, picked up the drone. The two left, Susan locked the front door.

"Calm down." Susan knew Pewter and Tucker well enough to chastise them. "You are not getting in my car until you calm down."

"Come on, you two. I'm ready to go home," Mrs. Murphy complained.

Tucker sat down then stood up, walking over to Mrs. Murphy. *"She started it."*

"She called you a mean name. Ignore it. We'll sit here for hours. You know how stubborn Susan can be. Walk to the station wagon with me and don't look back."

The two walked to Susan's Audi wagon. She had the back door open as well as the tailgate, Pirate needed the big space in the back. He could squeeze in Harry's vehicles, erratically cleaned by Harry. Susan was fanatical though.

Finally, all four animals inside, the two humans slid into the front, Susan turned on the motor.

Before driving out, she glanced around. "Looks good. Looks wonderful. I hope the dogwoods bloom for the ceremony. They're late this year, so maybe we'll get lucky. What do you think?"

"Hope so." Harry stretched out her legs. "I check and double-check stuff. You never know. I'm trying to have a backup plan for it all, but things do come right out of the blue. However, I can't goose the dogwoods along."

"Out of the blue, like a skeleton in a car."

"Exactly. Here comes Armand."

Susan, recognizing the new Range Rover, stopped, put down her window. "Are you being nosy?"

"Yes. I was hoping I'd find you. Called the house. Ned said you and Harry were here."

"Trying to think of everything," Harry told him.

"My question to you: Where are you going to serve the food, set up tables and chairs?" Armand half leaned out the window.

"The speeches will be in the front. We have an acre available, so we thought the tables, food, and drinks could be here." Susan pointed to the area, sweeping her hand toward the schools.

"What if it rains?" It was the sensitive question.

"We've ordered huge tents, the kind used for weddings, special outdoor fundraisers." Harry spoke over Susan's chest as she tried to muster eye contact with Armand.

"That will be attractive."

"We'll decorate the inside with huge ribbons in the school colors."

He nodded in appreciation. "Girls, you all, your husbands, have done so much. I haven't done a thing."

"Armand, we didn't expect you to. A lot of times you're out of the country. You run a big business."

He grinned. "Profit is a language understood in any country. My father taught me that. I came by to tell you I'm picking up the catering bill."

Susan, thrilled, replied, "Generosity is a language understood in any country, too."

He blew a kiss, put up his window, backed out, and drove off.

They both exclaimed in unison, "Oh my God."

Pewter hopped onto the center divider. *"You two are loud."* Then she dropped onto Harry's lap.

"Let's call Taz." Susan grappled for her cellphone, dialed Tazio, got her, so Susan and Harry happily babbled with her.

As Susan clicked off, Harry thought a moment. "That's a couple of thousand dollars of contribution."

"Yes, it is. He makes so much money, according to my husband, in international trade. He's low-key about it. I know he gives money to his church, but he doesn't draw attention to himself."

"Okay, but we can make sure he is thanked from the podium. A simple thank-you. We got lucky."

10

May 13, 2024

Monday

Overhead, the sky, a deep baby blue, made Harry feel this was heaven. A few angel-white cumulus clouds completed the effect. Riding the 50 horsepower John Deere tractor, bush-hogging didn't feel like a chore in these conditions. She and Fair had traded in an older, less powerful Ford tractor to buy this one—used, of course. Their big tractor would be much too big for this job.

The fragrance of the newly cut grass added to the pleasure of this early afternoon. The dogs and cats remained at the farm. She didn't want to worry about them as she prepared the acres behind the school. Years ago, when she was in her twenties, Harry was over at Aunt Tally's to pick up and clean her winter horse blankets. In her late seventies then, bordering on eighty, Aunt Tally still rode regularly. A hired hand was cutting the fields and as Harry stepped out of the barn, she saw a piece of a bush-hog blade fly off. The tractor was close enough to the barn, so the heavy broken blade slammed into the side of the barn. A person, dog, horse, you name it, would have been cut in two by the force of it.

She and the driver, a spindly older fellow named Swoop, ran to the side of the barn. They looked at each other. Equipment breaks. A blade breaking isn't all that unusual, but given the thickness of them, it doesn't happen all that often. You never know what you can't see when mowing. A rock could wiggle up over the years, the blade hits it. So the two of them stood there, eyes bugging out at how the broken blade lodged into the side of the barn.

Swoop whistled. "Jesus."

Harry answered, "Lucky. We're lucky."

Bumping along now, she thought back to that, which was why she'd left the animals at home. They'd been in a snit about it, but her dogs especially concerned her. They followed. Tucker stayed at a distance but anything could happen. Harry didn't mind the dogs following her if she was dragging the spider wheel tedder after cutting hay, or if she was rolling hay. The big round spider wheels, easily seen, provided little danger. Nor did the hay baler, which was guaranteed to break at least once every hay season. Harry was convinced the devil invented the hay baler. Although when it worked, it shortened the task.

Turning, slowing the tractor, she looked behind her. While the twenty acres to the rear of the school hadn't been fertilized in years, the grass, weedy but not awful, emitted the fabulous fragrance of cut grass. Moving along at a slightly faster pace, she inhaled deeply. She was sure she could find some people to buy round bales for their cattle. This wasn't good enough to be horse hay, but she could make a little money for the school.

Why hadn't she thought of this as they restored the buildings? She cursed herself, but then eased up because the work on the buildings and the immediate grounds had taken years, much labor, and no little cost. The work of stripping, scrubbing, painting alone was expensive.

Reaching the end of the rectangular twenty acres, back where the two old roads made a T, neither one much used, she turned right. Following what she believed to be the property line, she then turned right again to come down the northern side of the field. About halfway finished, she studied her work as the day moved along. In the old days, right up to the closing of the schools, the football and baseball fields had been back here. The school, full of athletes well coached by Moses Evenfall, made good use of their land. They kept it up themselves. Neither the county nor Crozet was going to give them the money for groundsmen. She slowed again, cut the motor, having heard a little crack.

She had moved about five feet since the noise. Kneeling down, she spied the top of a large piece of quartz. Secure in the earth, it wouldn't dislodge without a shovel. A later chore. What she did know was that she now had a nick in the blade. Wouldn't be that hard to smooth out. Grateful that the bush-hog hadn't been compromised, she climbed back up, knowing to cut a circle around this spot. She had been careful. One large branch needed to be hauled off, but that would mean tying a chain or heavy rope, attaching it to the back of the tractor, bush-hog removed. She'd need Fair for that.

Another hour and the job was done. The place looked renewed.

She said to herself, "Nothing a little love can't fix."

In front of the buildings rested the 2007 farm dually, a long flatbed attached to it by a gooseneck. It was the same truck she used for hauling horses. A ramp secured at the back of the flatbed was down. She lifted the bush-hog, grateful for modern technology, hit those two tracks, and drove up onto the flatbed. Cutting the motor, she then had to secure the tractor with three heavy yet somewhat stretchable flat ropes. That took some time and effort. Sweating, she stopped after flipping up the ramp and securing it. She opened the driver's door of the truck, started the motor, and ran down the windows. Then she turned off the motor, opened the extended cab door, pulled out a small cooler, and grabbed a cold iced tea. Walking back to sit on the flatbed, she thought this tea was the best cold tea she had ever drunk. Looking at the buildings, smelling the cut grass, and being Harry, she cataloged in her mind everything left to be done. She felt a surge of pride. Her eyes moistened. How hard they had worked, physically and politically. Taking another slug of tea, she said a prayer of thanks. It could have been so much worse. A motor alerted her.

Turning off the paved road, an old Firebird pulled up.

Out stepped Moses Evenfall. "Don't you know when to stop?"

"This place needs to be perfect. And what are you doing out here, driving that cool car?"

He lifted a shoulder, a half shrug. "Can't bear to part with it. Cruised around in this car when I was in my prime. Bench seats, so I could drape my arm around Sherry. I still like to drape my arm around her."

They both laughed.

"Have a thought," Harry said.

A look of fear crossed his face and they laughed some more.

"Here's my thought," Harry continued. "How about you walk around back with me and show me where the football field was and the baseball diamond?"

"Oh Lord, that is a walk down memory lane." He smiled, held up his hand so she could take it and leap down.

Harry chugged the last of that divine iced tea. "Coach Evenfall, I have more in my cooler. Would you like a drink?"

"No thanks. Come on, let me show you the field of champions."

They walked behind the buildings.

He stopped and lifted his arm. "Both fields were sited north–south, to keep the sun out of the players' eyes. The coach who preceded me, back in the thirties, was a country boy, so he was thinking about not only the sun but how to keep the fields as playable as possible." He pointed toward the northwest corner. "That's where the baseball field was. Bleachers on both sides. Backstop, we built ourselves right there, maybe forty feet from the corner of the land. Now, come up here halfway. See where that sweet gum tree is on the other side? That was the farthest goalpost, and the other one was up here, closer to the buildings. In 1959, the bleachers were the first thing to go. The city council of Crozet was offered money for them and took it. Jim Sanburne wasn't yet mayor. But it's not like anyone was pocketing cash. It went toward building a new library one day, which didn't happen until September 28, 2013, but that's okay. No one ever dreamed this place would come back. Can you imagine hundreds of people here, screaming their lungs out?"

"I can." She beamed up at him. It was impossible not to like Moz Evenfall.

"Do you need me to show you anything at the basketball court?"

"Think we've got that. The floor isn't bad, all things considered. Could be brought back. You know it's used in the winter for training show dogs. Linda King and Sam Ewing give clinics for Irish Wolfhounds, and some other AKC people give judging clinics. Very popular."

"People love their dogs. I couldn't live without my little Cash." He paused. "Cashew. Everyone calls their dogs Peanut, so I decided to use Cashew. Sherry said I was crazy. I reminded her she married me, so who is really crazy?" He laughed.

"Great name. Well, how about I round up some people on our committee and we lay out the diamond and the football field? All we have to do is walk behind two wheeled line layers. Nothing rigorous."

"You need to lay it out with flags first." He squinted, studying the land. "I'll tell you what, I'll come out here. Give me a day, a weekend is probably best, but I can round up some fellows and we'll do it. You all can lay down the chalk. We've even used sawdust in a pinch. Course, these days those lines are often painted. You don't want to do that. Will be expensive and the walk behind is different. If you can get the chalk, that would be just fine, and it will last until the celebration, even after the celebration."

"Good. Who knows, maybe kids will come back here and use the baseball diamond. We don't have enough parks. I guess kids go to the high school or middle school, but that's not the same," she replied.

"You're right. We need more places where people can come together and relax. Not you. You're out there on that big farm, but most people live in towns, cities, suburbs."

"I wouldn't mind finding friends at a park. I get a kick out of watching kids play, no matter what they are playing . . . or adults, for that matter. You know Waynesboro has a baseball team, men's? I like to watch them play. The drive to Richmond to see the Braves wears me out."

"Tell you what, I wouldn't play on artificial turf, no matter what they paid me. Better to play on this field right here, unattended as it has been. Nothing like real turf underfoot." He crossed his arms over his chest. "Oh, Harry, those were the days. We worked together. Yes, we were segregated, but we coaches often got together, white and Black. Everybody knew everybody and we all knew who had talent. Didn't matter if it was Warrenton or Richmond or Winchester. If there was a good athlete, white or Black, we knew. When I look back, I realize despite all, I have led a charmed life. I worked with great people and, thank God, I married a good woman. Best thing I ever did. I look around now and I don't see that closeness. I'm older than dirt, but wouldn't be young now for anything. Sherry and I talk about it a lot."

"Fair and I do, too. Course, we didn't live through as much as you all did, but we've seen enough, and Aunt Tally takes me on trips down memory lane."

"Haven't seen the old girl in years. How's she doing?"

"She's frail. Can't ride anymore, but her eyesight is still good. Hearing is good. Moving slow, but moving. She's going to come to the ceremony."

"Be wonderful to see her. Sherry was telling me, she reads the news on her phone, about the dead man found in Aunt Tally's creek.

Been there for years, and you and that fella found it? Had to be a jolt."

"Was. I was testing the drone Fair bought for me. Lucas, who works for Aunt Tally, wanted to check the farm road on the other side of the creek. The road needs help. Much of it has washed away over the years. It was raining but not awful, so I sent the thing up, and that's how we found the car. Could see the back bumper in the water. We called Cooper. The department sent out people. Nothing much going on that weekend so it wasn't a long wait, and when they pulled up the car, water running out of it, that's when we saw the skeleton in the driver's seat. Funny. You don't know whether to scream or run. We stood there dumbfounded. Big ugh."

"The news said he was a geology professor. And it may be murder."

"That's what Cooper says. The forensic team believes he was shot through the heart, based on the damage to his ribs. The only good thing about that is it had to be fast."

"I guess."

The two of them walked back to the vehicles.

"So, Coach, what do you want for that Firebird?" She smiled at him.

"People ask me that all the time. Not for sale. If we need to go on a long trip, we use Sherry's Camry. Nice car."

"Yes, it is. Who can get a loan for a car today?"

Shaking his head, Coach Evenfall answered, "Not me. I'm not paying that interest rate. Do you know, Harry, I couldn't buy my own house today."

"Me neither." She thought to herself how that seemed to be people's first response to the cost of things.

A rumble alerted them. A dually with "Munson and Sons" on the side pulled up.

"Saw your Firebird. Hi, Harry, Moz, what are you doing back here?"

"Being nosy. Saw your building over there in Far Fields. You and the boys never stop working."

Arch Munson grinned. "We do our best to meet deadlines. The problem with construction is, delays cost even more than the price of materials." He looked at Harry. "Given all that you did here, I don't have to tell you."

"We did a little at a time. Did much of it ourselves."

"More power to ya." Arch looked around. "I left school here when I was in the seventh grade in 1959. A different world."

"Was," Moz simply agreed. "Maybe you did go to a school with new athletic equipment, new books, but you weren't exactly wanted."

Arch shrugged. "I said to myself, 'The hell with them.'"

"Sounds awful." Harry thought it was.

"Harry, you can get used to anything. Once I reached sixteen, I'd filled out, did well in junior varsity, and my junior and senior years I played halfback. Everybody loved me then."

"You made All State." Moz patted the side of the truck. "Think we'll set out the baseball diamond and football field. Come on back after the reconstruction."

"Boy, that will bring back memories." Arch looked toward the field, what he could see. "Sandy Rycroft keeps talking about putting up expensive houses back there. Terrific location, but it doesn't seem right to replace the school."

"Glad you feel that way," Harry chimed in.

"We'd make a bundle, but me and the boys are doing okay. Well, back to work."

Harry and Coach chatted a bit more as Arch drove away, then Coach got into his supercar and took off.

Harry double-checked how secure the tractor was, gunned up the big truck, managed to drive a circle to turn around, and home she went.

As she opened her house's back door, Pewter, sprawled on the kitchen table, looked up, unrepentant. *"Did you bring me anything?"*

11

May 14, 2024

Tuesday

Cooper rubbed her eyes as she sat in front of her home computer. She had been in the patrol car most of the day. When she got home she'd wanted to dip into more research.

The rain outside helped her concentrate.

Denver Raiselle's case intrigued her. For one thing, she knew nothing about geology. As he was a geologist, she thought his career might explain, if nothing else, his pattern of thinking.

He'd been found four days earlier. The more she searched increased the chance, a slim chance, that something might guide her in the right direction.

What the sheriff's department had gathered was how well liked he was.

Going back through bank accounts, his income was certainly enough to pay his bills, the family's, and leave a bit for a vacation annually. He didn't spend money on cars, expensive items. The vacations remained in this country. Also, which she carefully noted, his vacations were often to national parks dovetailed with geology. The family visited the Grand Canyon. He studied the rock striations visually, right there. Another time they traveled to Georgia, the end of the Appalachian Trail . . . or the beginning, depending on which direction you were hiking. Often they pitched a tent. These joys could be spontaneous, unlike today, when one had to make a reservation with park services. Without a doubt, life was becoming more circumscribed, more controlled.

She knew if an illegal activity pulled in the cash, all had to be hidden. However, her gut told her Raiselle was what he seemed, a nice guy who loved his work.

His focus had been the slate seam throughout Virginia. Ancillary to that, Cooper found herself studying the formations of the Blue Ridge Mountains, created by tectonic plates uplifting 1.1 billion to 250 million years ago. Like so many people, she took the beautiful mountains for granted, not realizing they were among the oldest in the world. Some scientists say they were second only to the Barberton Greenstone Belt in South Africa. Others argued that, no, they were really third, behind the Black Hills in South Dakota and Wyoming. However, no one disputed that they were blue, thanks to the isoprene released in the atmosphere by all those beautiful trees. The mountain belt, rich in a variety of trees as well as creatures, running from the last Ice Age, caught her attention. How could she get through Virginia Tech and not learn these things?

Scrolling, she stopped to absorb that the northeast to southwest orientation was what allowed species to migrate 10,000 years ago, the last Ice Age. The dividing zone between a northern climate and a southern one sat for ten miles on top of the Blue Ridge in Nelson County, the county adjoining Albemarle. That astonished her.

What also astonished her was how much Denver knew, studied, and wrote. The temperate climate of the area also gave creatures an advantage as they fled from the north. She shivered unexpectedly. Those bitter spells in January and February seemed hateful. What could it have been in an Ice Age? Humans were on earth long before then.

To her surprise, she learned that the Blue Ridge rose one hundred feet every million years, which was an advantage. The top of the range would remain a bit cooler than below.

Leaning back in her chair, she rubbed her eyes again, her admiration for the deceased man growing. Why would anyone kill someone this educated? Over slate?

After the war, Richmond, shattered, needed to rebuild. General Schofield, put in charge of this huge task, learned of the slate seam running through the Piedmont. A large quarry located at Penlan Station provided for the city. The railroad tracks stopped at the quarry, making it easier to haul tons of slate into town.

This particular slate, high grade, containing flecks of mica, was impervious to the elements and easily lasted one hundred and fifty years, more if well kept.

Denver's specialty was the thermal metamorphose, the andalusite crystal created by this event. He knew the history, from creation to modern use.

Rubbing her eyes once more, she thought that the victim's geological interest combined with the rebuilding of Richmond surely made his research fascinating. To this day, slate shingles were durable, beautiful, and expensive. She'd learned this from Harry, in charge of building and grounds at St. Luke's Lutheran Church. Every now and then, Harry needed to replace shingles, slate, on the roof of the large church and its outbuildings. Originally built immediately after the Revolutionary War, the church still had its shingles.

Clicking off her computer, she felt she hadn't wasted time but she also hadn't scraped up any information pointing toward friction in Denver's life.

Using the computer at work, she was more disciplined. Here at home she could stray into extraneous subjects.

She had learned that Professor Raiselle was an expert in his field.

And she had to admit thinking about the age of the Blue Ridge Mountains, how they were formed, the special properties of shale, was interesting.

She picked up her phone and dialed. "Harry."

"Hey. How are you? I'm doing the laundry. How's that for excitement?"

"You can come do mine," Cooper teased her. "Did you know the orientation of the Blue Ridge Mountains allowed species to travel along the spine to escape the Ice Age ten thousand years ago?"

"No, I did not."

"I've been cruising my computer, geology. Curious because of the murder victim. Found out a lot of interesting stuff, but nothing that might lead to murder. Just a thought."

"That's the problem with sitting alone at home. You swear you'll do research and the next thing you know, you've learned everything about Rita Hayworth or the Battle of Midway." She laughed.

"Hey, I gave it a try."

"What's popping up in your garden?"

"Corn. Beginnings of tomato stalks. I check every day."

"Speaking of checking, what if you and I went back to Aunt Tally's to send my drone in the other direction? I bet we find sites where a car could have been dumped."

"Okay. I can meet you there tomorrow afternoon if it's not raining. I'll tell Rick. Pretty sure he'll let me go, as it's legit."

12

May 15, 2024

Wednesday

The whirr of the drone faded as Harry and Cooper watched the screen.

"Stop," Cooper ordered as she bent closer to the screen. "What do you think?"

Harry noted the bridge on the adjoining farm, downstream. "You could push a car into the water. A farm bridge isn't traveled as much as a state road bridge."

"A farm bridge would only work if it wasn't much used. Look at Aunt Tally's main bridge today. Lucas is getting up the rest of her hay, Blue Ridge Farmers Coop delivered feed plus seed bags. Someone would notice tire tracks, unless rain washed them out. It seems to me a place would either have to be on an unused or barely used road, or one that has a lot of daytime traffic, not much at night. People concentrate on going to work. They can miss what's right under their noses."

"I suppose." Harry sent the drone farther down in a westward direction then brought it back. The device set down right in front of her.

"For the hell of it, send this to the border of my land with Aunt Tally's. At the narrow dividing stream. The one that feeds into Swift Creek."

"Okay."

Again the two women observed the path.

"Beavers," Harry noted.

"I don't mind them." Cooper looked at how impressive the beaver lodge was. "A high-rise."

"Right." Harry laughed. "I've got them on the creek dividing your land and mine. Beaver, muskrats, great blue herons."

"Every species has its special skills. Okay, bring it back."

As the drone again returned, Harry shut it off. "It's amazing what you can see."

"It is. Although we don't know any more than when we started."

"Did you expect to?"

"No. But I was hopeful. I have to keep hope or I'd walk away from cases fresh and old. Fortunately, there aren't that many unsolved murders in the county. The ones we do have predate DNA testing for the most part." Cooper put her thumb in her belt.

"Come on. Let's go back to my farm. Actually, I have a better idea. Let's go to the school. I want to see the acres behind it again."

"Okay."

To keep the peace, Harry stopped at her farm to pick up her four-footed friends. The beat-up old Volvo station wagon could fit everyone in it.

"Harry, you've got close to 200,000 miles on this thing."

"I know. Fair has his dually, has his meds and stuff in it. I've got the 1978 Ford F-150 and this. I rarely count the flatbed dually. We use that to haul big stuff on the farm. Really, you need a car and a truck on a farm. Who wants to pull a dually into a parking place or an old Ford? It's gotten to the point where I drive the truck and people want to buy it. Right then and there. The other day I gave Moz Evenfall a halfway offer for his Firebird."

"Ha. He's kept that thing in top shape. I think this is an age divider. I mean, those who are middle-aged remember when cars were part of our personality. I'm not so sure the young feel that way."

"They do if they own Teslas." Harry lifted an eyebrow.

"You're right. Electric cars make a lot of sense if you live in the city. Otherwise, no. Not enough chargers, lose about twenty percent of your power when the temperature drops below freezing. Add a high grade to that and you lose more power. Here we are in the foothills of the Blue Ridge Mountains, we crisscross the mountains once or twice a week. It'll never work. Electric vehicles won't work for the sheriff's department either."

"I bet the manufacturers will figure out how to make an electric police car."

Cooper turned around. "Maybe. They'd have to reinforce it, because we get in crashes more than regular drivers. A car chase is terrifying, not exciting. You pray someone isn't going to pull in front of you, or stay in your way, and you know whoever you are chasing doesn't give a damn about human life. Some of the most gruesome stuff I have seen has been the result of a car chase." She turned around. "Tucker has a banana."

"That's her new special toy. It's a stuffed banana, looks real from a distance."

"Is this the new hot item?"

"Yes, it is."

"Selfish. Selfish. Selfish," Pewter informed Cooper as she sat in the backseat with Mrs. Murphy, Tucker, and even Pirate, who'd wedged himself in.

Cooper laughed. "Wouldn't it be great if a stuffed banana made you that happy?"

"I'll take a pig's ear," Pirate said.

"That is so gross." Pewter wanted the banana not because she thought it was special but because Tucker wanted it.

"Here we are." Harry pulled in, noticing a new Lexus parked in front of the high school.

"You've been mowing." Cooper got out.

"Doing it once a week. I'll need to mow the back one more time. I wonder who's here."

"Bet we find out."

They walked around the buildings, and sure enough, Sandy Rycroft was walking over the back acres. Seeing the two women, he waved, walked toward them.

Tucker, having left her banana in the car, barked, as did Pirate.

"You two stay." The cats stayed, too.

"Harry, Cooper. It looks good back here," Sandy complimented Harry, who he knew was one of the mainstays on the restoration committee.

"Thanks. This weekend Moz Evenfall and some of his buddies are going to lay out the site of the old football and baseball fields. They'll remember better than anyone. Susan and I will lay down the chalk lines. Should bring back old times."

"I'm sure it will. I bet there will be a big crowd. This is good for Crozet."

"How's business?" Harry asked.

"Good. Still getting cash offers for some of the big estates, some also in the middle. As you know, the interest rates have slowed sales down. A lot of older people would like to move to smaller places but aren't selling because the house they own is low interest. This has caused a generational jam. That's how I think of it."

"Never thought of that," Harry confessed.

"Well, I have." Cooper smiled.

"You bought the Jones homeplace." Sandy, like every realtor, knew what had sold and to whom.

"Yes. My mortgage papers numbered about thirty. Thought I would go blind from reading."

Sandy laughed. "If you bought it today, it would be forty pages. But what we have here is such wonderful natural beauty: University of Virginia in Charlottesville, the junior college, plus Mary Baldwin over the mountain, and good restaurants. Lots of activities, especially if one likes the outdoors. Business is slower, but it never stops. People want to leave a big city, they see this place, and that does it. Nonetheless, I recognize there is a cyclical aspect. When the market is hot, I don't delude myself into thinking it's always going to be that way. That was a lesson I learned the hard way. I never thought I'd take over Dad's business. After all, I was a Russian major in college. But here I am running the business. I've learned to like it despite hard lessons."

"Those are the lessons you never forget." Cooper nodded.

"Before I forget," Sandy turned to Harry, "I'd like to talk to the restoration committee. Nothing long-winded."

"I'll check with the group. We have weekly meetings, so we can probably fit you in."

Tucker and Pirate stuck close with Harry while the cats trotted to the back of the schoolhouse.

"*Have you noticed people never talk about catnip?*" Pewter peered along the foundation.

"*Harry has mentioned catnip tea, plus she gives us catnip.*"

"*You're right, but she doesn't discuss it with other people. They talk about farming, equipment, money. I don't think they live through their senses. Just a thought. Aha.*" Pewter stopped in front of a mouse hole through the basement foundation logs.

The school was built before concrete blocks were readily available.

"*Clever. Wonder if that was chewed open back when the school was built,*" Mrs. Murphy posed.

"*I could push dirt over it.*"

"*It's better if they can come and go. If any mice were trapped in these buildings they'd run from the people on the big day. Scare the mice and scare the people. Best they stay hidden. So don't stop up the hole."*

"Okay," Pewter agreed. *"Why do some people scream when they see mice?"*

"I have no idea. Stuff sets them off. Like when Harry hears a song she likes, she has to sing along with it or dance if she's cleaning the house. Things stick in their minds. She's not at all afraid of mice, or most any animal, but I can always tell when there's people she doesn't like."

"She doesn't much care for Sandy Rycroft," Pewter noted.

"Yeah. She doesn't dislike him, but she's wary," Mrs. Murphy agreed.

Harry and Cooper returned to the old station wagon as Harry described to her friend what they hoped to accomplish over the weekend.

Everyone settled in and Harry started the motor. "What could I say?"

"Nothing. Just call everyone. It's better you all hear whatever he's got on his mind."

"If he wants a meeting with us, it has to be over the schools."

"He's a realtor. He'll pitch something."

"Makes my head ache. He'll come up with some kind of development idea."

"Perhaps he wants to create a new neighborhood close to here. There's still some land available. Might have to knock down an old house, but there's places nearby. Maybe he wants to use the name."

"Maybe. Wonder if I should call Jim Sanburne."

"Wait until you know what he wants. Which reminds me, when is the last time you've seen Big Mim?"

"Maybe two weeks ago at Aunt Tally's." Harry rolled down the driveway. "Why?"

"She looks really good. Got a touch-up."

"You think so?"

"Either that or she's sleeping fourteen hours a night." Cooper laughed.

Harry laughed with her. "She has the money. It is tempting. Could you ever do it?"

"Probably. If I reached a point where my face made me feel older than I wish, yeah. There are alternatives now. You don't have to go under the knife."

Harry shivered. "I don't know. If you don't get a true facelift then don't you have to keep doing stuff like Botox throughout the year?"

"I think so. And I bet all of it hurts."

"Yeah. I'm a big chicken."

"If they had fur, none of this would be a problem. My face will be eternally young," Pewter purred.

"That's because you're fat," Tucker sassed.

A donnybrook ensued. Harry pulled the car over.

"Stop it. I mean it."

Cooper started laughing. "They're worse than kids."

"It's her fault," Pewter screeched.

Pirate looked out the window. Mrs. Murphy sat between his paws as Tucker and Pewter went at it.

"Tucker, give me your banana."

"Oh no." Tucker appeared stricken.

Harry got out of the car, opened the back door. "I'm taking this banana. And Pewter, if I hear one peep out of you, no treats tonight. I mean it."

Harry climbed back into the driver's seat, the banana on her lap.

"That banana looks so valuable." Cooper grinned.

Harry picked it up before starting the car, handing it to Cooper. "You can protect it."

"If bananas were all we had to worry about, we'd have a good life."

Harry started laughing. "You're right."

Fifteen minutes later, Harry turned onto Cooper's farm road. "You've got a bloom on your grandiflora magnolia. Early."

"A bloom, a banana, younger than springtime. Remember that song?"

"Sort of. Mom would play those show tunes. Spring has been terrific, song or not. I say let's take our pleasures where we can."

"I'm with you."

Harry pulled up to Cooper's back door. "Hey, if you want to borrow the drone, let me know."

"Thanks." Cooper looked in the backseat. "Very quiet. That would worry me more than the noise."

Cooper had a point there.

13

May 16, 2024

Thursday

Hung on the large corkboard in Tazio's office was a map of the schools as well as the acres in the back. Next to the map was a topo map from the U.S. Geological Survey. These maps are colored and expensive, but also accurate, useful. The size of a topo map allows one to see more than you would crawling through a computer model. Also on the map are distinguishing features, land gradations.

Tazio, Harry, Susan, Fair, and Lucas, the restoration group, focused on the maps. Ned hadn't been able to make it. He was in Richmond, although the Assembly had adjourned. There was lots of work to do whether in session or out of it.

Everyone watched Sandy Rycroft as he pointed to each map with a wooden ruler, twelve inches. He wore a tweed jacket and a tie, looking relaxed but professional. Sandy greatly resembled his father, who always looked proper. He knew this group would be difficult to convince to aid in his purchasing the fifteen acres behind the school buildings. He stayed factual, not raising his voice. The less emotion, the better, he thought.

"You can see the two farm roads at the back. These would be graded, widened, and covered in asphalt. The company would pay, of course."

Harry made a mental note to drive those roads, starting from the state road. The longest state road, which ran north to south, was perhaps a mile from the farm roads. The east–west road, maybe a half mile from the farm roads. She'd check her mileage meter. The state road, the north–south, was the route into Crozet from Route 250 or coming from White Hall, depending upon which direction you traveled. That road and the shorter east–west one were well maintained by the state. Good roads make for happy citizens. Any contractor considering a development had to factor in constant road maintenance by the development. The state didn't take care of development roads. They did a good job on the state roads though, which winter could tear up.

Susan watched Sandy's presentation with her grandfather's wisdom echoing in her head. "Find out who the investors are. They will tell you if people will keep their word. If you can't find out, including the so-called silent partners, don't do business with them. Same for candidates. Who's pouring in the money?"

Lucas, also politically shrewd, thought along lines similar to Susan.

Tazio knew Sandy Rycroft's real estate company. As an architect, she often worked for people to whom he'd sold houses or farms. He did not hide faults or expenses, such as a house needing a new roof. He also gave clients a list of inspectors to go over the property before a deal was signed. Her experience was that he was up-front. Her experience also was that he was a salesman, a personality type she encountered whether in real estate or with stockbrokers. She betrayed no signs of liking or disliking his pitch.

Fair remained neutral. He wasn't a businessman. He was a scientist really. All veterinarians are. But he listened carefully.

"So five acres behind the buildings remain with the schools." He pointed to the map. "This fifteen would be fenced off, used as common land for the homes built around the perimeter of the property . . . like Manhattan's Gramercy Park, in a way. Everyone gets land to walk on, use, maintained by the homeowners association. No one has to do any work. The land would also be attractive for the schools, as nothing would be built on it, only on the edges."

He rattled on, giving a good presentation. Then he hung the drawings over the map and topo map on the corkboard.

"Come up and look more closely." He stepped back.

Tazio, the first out of her chair, looked over the map. She was quickly joined by the rest of the restoration group.

Harry asked the first question. "The creek floods from time to time. How do you anticipate fixing that?"

"We'll put in a big culvert at the corner, the western corner, so we can build a simple bridge and the east–west road will be extended."

"The whole way to Chiles Orchard?" Susan was incredulous.

"No. To connect to the first road, which is a development road to the west of here. Not far. That gives those residents a back way out, as well as a quicker way to Chiles Orchard. If you go in the other direction, you'll get on the main road to the Crozet Post Office. We're still working on that."

Lucas stated, "So the fifteen acres are really a private park for the residences."

"Yes, just like Gramercy Park, but much smaller, of course." He smiled.

"How many houses?" Tazio asked.

"Thirty to thirty-five, and that leaves space between each home, enough for the owners to plant whatever bushes, flowers, and a tree or two if they wish. We considered building the units with common walls to save space and energy, but decided against that. We won't truly know the number of houses until we own the land and can accurately measure."

"And the rooftops?" Tazio was zeroing in.

"Slate. Yes, we will have a design protocol. Nothing modern. The style has to be Federal or Georgian. Not even Victorian. The effect will be peaceful, harmonious, nothing jarring in material or color. Every home will have a fireplace. The wood will cause more pollution but people love true fireplaces, and given how often we lose power out here, having one offers some protection."

"Gas?" Susan asked.

"No. A true woodburning fireplace. Other than that, plus the design, all the materials are the latest . . . the insulation, no plastics on the floor. Natural substances. The stoves will be electric."

Harry piped up, "That's no good when the power is out."

"No, it isn't, but Federal pressure is ramping up about stoves." Sandy's distaste was obvious. "You all may not agree, but I firmly do not believe the government can tell us what to buy. I believe in alternatives for when the power cuts out. Some of the storms we have been having these last few years are fierce. Most people will have generators when the power is out. They, too, pollute."

The others nodded in agreement.

Then Tazio asked, "You could put in gas stoves."

"True, but the banks are uneasy," he honestly replied. "We need the banks both for our buyers and for ourselves, should we need more money. We'll put in electric stoves. I bring that up because even though we have solid financing, you never know."

"That's the truth," Harry agreed.

"While we are on that subject, who is financing this?" Susan asked what the others were thinking, again remembering her grandfather's wisdom.

"Thanatos has put up a small amount. We, Hickory Real Estate, will utilize our relationships at the local banks plus put up some of our own money. Investors are waiting for a clean sale."

Lucas learned from Amanda, even when they were in college, to be meticulous about money. Her political career started when she presented her district with a detailed account of state waste, most especially for her district. Amanda won in a landslide and she continued her financial prudence once in office. The woman never once turned in a sloppy account.

"What do you estimate to be the total cost?" Lucas asked.

"For the purchase of the fifteen acres, upgrading the farm roads that have a built-in right-of-way, and laying out each lot, we believe the cost will be eleven million dollars if done today. If inflation still plagues us, the amount goes up."

"Why are you pitching it to us?" Susan, shrewd, went right for it.

"Because if you all are opposed, this will be much harder to effect. We think this will be a wonderful addition to Crozet. We will divide the purchase price to the town over four years. This helps them with taxes . . . and us as well."

"What happens should you fail?" Fair surprised everyone with his question.

"It all reverts back to Crozet if we fail before people are living in the houses. After they buy, it's up to the homeowners association."

"Again, why are you pitching this to us?" Tazio repeated Susan's question.

"You have transformed an eyesore. It will be used by the county for historical lessons. It will probably have a historical plaque given by the state. And we offer each of you one hundred and fifty thousand dollars for your work. Free and clear. You only need to sign a document avowing you will not work against the project. It will be simple. The money for this development will do a great deal for Crozet. We have our problems here. Not a lot, but this is a fund for a rainy day. Considering the weather, that's probably the best term for it, as none of us have any idea what's happening economically long-term."

The conversation continued for another forty-five minutes, then Sandy left. Susan told him they would get back to him within the week.

Everyone grabbed a drink from Lucas's Yeti chest.

"Well?" Tazio looked at each person.

"Why now?" Harry wondered. "We know realtors, developers, have been sniffing around the school since we were halfway finished with our task, but why now?"

Lucas pushed back a lock of blond hair, took a drink of cold sweet tea. "Maybe because everyone's eyes will be on the school thanks to the celebration. It might embolden those who want to fatten Crozet's treasury."

"And he offered us money." Harry was incensed.

"Think of it as the cost of our labors . . . which, by the way, is not high enough." Susan smiled.

Fair lifted his hands, palms upward. "I'm confused. Do any of you think this is a real offer?"

"Actually, I do," Lucas calmly replied. "Offers for this land will come and go over the years. Who knows what will happen twenty years from now or even ten? And who knows what will happen when Jim isn't mayor anymore."

"We should have tried to buy it from the city." Tazio furrowed her brow.

"Oh well, nobody wanted it, and the city didn't want it either until we started working on it. Then they couldn't make up their mind to sell. But Tazio, where would we have gotten the money?" Susan stopped herself. "Actually, it's possible we could have raised it if we started a nonprofit, but how could we start a nonprofit without owning the land? I mean, of course we could, but it would seem like pie in the sky."

"So what do we do now?" Harry asked.

"Go to Jim Sanburne," her husband counseled. "We should listen to his ideas. He doesn't want to sell anything. You know that, but he will have insight."

"I'll see if I can get a meeting with him soon," Tazio offered.

"Good," came the chorus.

"I never saw this coming." Harry was so upset.

"I can't say it didn't occur to me. But not now, sometime down the road." Tazio spoke in an even tone of voice. "Greed."

"You know, I like Sandy. He's been a positive part of Crozet for years. I find it hard to believe he's the front man." Fair, too, was disturbed.

"He sure has a lot to gain," Lucas quietly said.

"Who knows what he has to lose?" That idea popped into Harry's head.

"What do you mean?" Susan knocked back a drink.

"I don't know," Harry answered. "But I do know sometimes people are working to protect themselves."

14

May 17, 2024

Friday

Harry, Susan, and Cooper, along with Mrs. Murphy, Pewter, Tucker, and Pirate, worked in the Jones family graveyard. Pewter chose to sit in the old sweet gum tree in the middle of the fifty-by-forty-foot graveyard. This was a big cemetery, but the Jones family had been in the county since 1790. Never rich, hardworking, they made it through farming. Their tombstones, neatly arranged, demonstrated the planning and care prior generations took with their ancestors. Nothing was out of place, the tombstones were all the same size and shape. Granite, three feet high, two feet wide. This allowed for ample room should the survivors wish to make a somewhat lengthy memory. The stonecutters used a Roman typeface with serifs.

Cooper had mowed the grass last night after work. So the women scrubbed the tombstones, as well as trimming the grass close to the stones.

"I never tire of Reverend Jones's grandfather's inscription," Harry stated as she scrubbed the letters then read it aloud. "'A love of the earth is the begining of virtue.'"

"I like this one from 1831. Joan Jones. 'An angel on earth now resides with our Heavenly Father.'"

"Lot of love in the Jones family." Cooper, on her knees, cleaned an infant's grave, which had a small, square stone set into the earth.

The large stones belonged to the adults.

"Yes. They've given a lot to Virginia." Susan stopped to take a breath. "Isn't it interesting how many of the old families still live here? Coles, Paynes, Randolphs, Cabells, and Alexanders, and that's just the beginning. There's something about our state. The young leave to make careers but so often they come back. There's one or two in every family who go. Well, there always were. Madison left for a while. Of course, travel took so long in the eighteenth century, up until trains, that if you went somewhere, you stayed a spell, as my grandmother says." Susan smiled, as her family was one that had been in Virginia since the 1630s.

Cooper stood up to unkink her legs. She was right under Pewter, who looked down.

"My family has been here forever," Pewter informed her. *"All over the world, I think we are among the oldest inhabitants."*

"Pewter, who cares?" Tucker, outside the cemetery, luxuriating in the grass, yipped.

"I like knowing." Pewter for once avoided a fight.

"Do they know?" Pirate indicated the three humans.

"Susan has no choice and Cooper only once or twice mentioned what they term their people. *Some humans set great store by this stuff."* Mrs. Murphy's tail flicked up and down at the very end.

Cooper surveyed their labors. "Well, this place looks good."

"Let me finish this last tombstone. I can barely make out the dates." Harry then read, "1841 to 1900. Boy, she lived through a lot."

"They all did." Susan also stood. "We're the vain ones thinking we're living through the most difficult times. Ego. All ego."

"Reverend Jones will be impressed." Cooper smiled.

"He'll say you should have told him and he would have hired workers. It's up to the family to tend to the graveyard. Virginia law states you can visit your family's resting place and tidy it all up. The owner can set restrictions on the frequency, hours, and duration of the visits. The lawn needs to be mowed. Fallen tombstones need to be righted. One can do those things." Susan removed her gardening gloves.

"He has no family left," Harry said. "Sad to make it through Vietnam, come back, study to be an Episcopal priest, but never have children. He's such a lovable man."

"Yes, he is. But you know, maybe with all he endured in the war—he was in heavy combat, remember—it kept him from the closeness most of us want. Then his wife died in middle age. That would be dreadful. I think about that sometimes, especially the war. Grandmother said sometimes it was difficult for my grandfather. A memory would jump up or he would awaken in the night, sweating. He was in the Army in World War II," Susan recalled. "Okay, I'm ready to sit in a chair for a minute. Let's put this stuff in the gator. You bought a big ATV from Wayne's Cycle Shop, Cooper."

"I did. I can do most of what I have to do here with this. I suppose someday I should buy a big truck, but right now I can move tools, buckets, water in jars. The ATV takes care of it and uses so little gas."

"Wish I could say the same." Harry put buckets, sponges, and Dawn dish cleaner in the small wagon hooked to the back of the ATV.

"You have a lot more to do," Cooper reminded her.

They clambered into the ATV, as did the cats. Pewter did not relish a walk back to the farmhouse. The dogs trotted along. Once back, the women put the tools away. Cooper had built a nice shed, since the old one from the forties listed to port.

Once that was accomplished, they all washed their hands with the outside hose. Cooper went in to fetch sandwiches she'd made that morning, while Harry and Susan brought the cooler from Susan's Audi wagon.

Chairs arranged outside, the table in the middle, they gratefully sat down to eat and drink. Harry provided special crunchies for the dogs and cats. The cats got Temptations, while the dogs got beef crunchies. Not a lot, but enough to keep them happy.

"Oh, I love this chair." Susan exhaled.

They basked as the light filtered through the trees by the house. Each caught up with the others' latest activities.

Susan told Cooper about Sandy Rycroft, as she knew Cooper would tell no one.

"What do you think?" Harry asked.

"Why now?" Cooper's mouth turned up. "I would guess other realtors have nosed around or even contacted Jim Sanburne directly."

"He doesn't speak of it, I think because no one made an offer in dollars. Probably was all just talk, but Sandy made an offer." Harry guzzled her Perrier with lime, perfect for the day.

"Is it a reasonable offer?" Cooper asked.

"In the ballpark, eleven million. I checked with my smart husband. But he, like us, finds this odd—the timing as well as offering money to those of us who did the work," Susan answered.

"And I say something's not right." Harry was adamant.

"Hickory Real Estate appears to be doing great; selling estates, plus lots in the developments. People are snapping properties up." Susan looked at Harry. "That doesn't mean you're wrong, but I can't think of what might be amiss. Sandy sure seems to have enough money."

"What if this isn't about money?" Harry looked back at her friend.

"Harry, everything is about money. Americans worship the Golden Calf."

Cooper interjected, "True, Susan, but there's stuff that set people on the wrong track or they hide. If there's one thing my job has taught me, it's that most everyone has secrets."

"I don't. What you see is what you get," Pewter, under Harry's chair, remarked.

"We see a lot." Tucker giggled.

Pewter hurried out from under the chair but Tucker was already running across the lawn.

"For a fat girl, she can move." Cooper laughed.

They watched the show with amusement while Mrs. Murphy and Pirate delicately accepted a few tidbits from the humans.

"Well, Coop, what kind of secret would be worth millions?" Harry got up to fetch another Perrier. "Anyone want a drink?"

"No," Cooper and Susan replied.

Susan plucked a brownie off her plate. "Political secrets that can derail a career, such as illegal income, misrepresenting property, debts, secret drug addiction. Actually, there's a long list. Don't forget infidelity. Could cost you money or your life."

"Well, we aren't going to stop any of it," Cooper wisely said.

"But what else? Murder? Some violent crime? Is Hickory Real Estate party to a large sin they committed with Thanatos Real Estate? I don't get it, I just don't get it. And furthermore, I am sure Jim Sanburne isn't going to entertain this offer." Harry spoke with conviction.

"I am pretty sure of that, too, but I'm curious." Susan looked at the late-afternoon light washing over the cemetery. "Golden. Just golden."

"Sure is. I've been reading that the Monacans buried some of their dead in mounds." Cooper mentioned this. "Got interested when we discovered that Denver Raiselle was Monacan, on his mother's side. In archaeology, the treatment of the dead is important. Think of the pyramids. Well, I prefer the peacefulness of the Jones's resting place."

"Me too. We put in a good day's work." Harry smiled.

Pewter sauntered back. "*Tucker is cowering in the garden.*"

Tucker, distracted by rabbit scent, wasn't cowering.

Harry looked at Cooper. "Is anyone going to bury Rasielle?"

Cooper said, "His wife will bury him out where she lives. Once the medical examiner is done, they'll send the bones. There's something about putting a body to rest. It's part of every civilization." Cooper finished her drink.

"*Antigone.*" Susan simply said the name of the play.

"Wandering souls." Harry picked up the thread. "People to this day believe wandering souls are those not properly put to rest or whose deaths have not been resolved. Oh, you know, people are in a house supposedly haunted and they see a fleeting figure in a hallway in the night."

"Do you believe it?" Cooper asked.

"I don't disbelieve it." Susan lifted her eyebrows.

"Maybe it's best we don't know. I don't believe in disturbing the dead, anyone dead," Harry avowed.

"Me neither, but finding a body isn't disturbing the dead. At least, I don't think it is. It allows the living to say a proper goodbye." Susan believed in the solace of knowing where your people rest.

"True." Cooper nodded. "But I think it only allows a proper goodbye if you know what happened. I want to know what happened to the professor. I'm not hopeful, but you never know."

15

May 18, 2024

Saturday

"Why do I listen to you? This was your idea." Susan carefully placed the first-base bag.

"You thought it was a good one." Harry pushed the small cart filled with lime. "I never thought laying a line took such patience. I thought I'd just walk along, knock it out."

"Remind me not to listen to you." Susan was on her hands and knees, laying chalk up to first base.

"Yeah, yeah." Harry, sweating, was not thrilled either, but she wasn't going to complain too much.

Moz and a group of men he had gathered, younger men, were meticulously measuring out the football field. Armand Neff worked with them. He said he hadn't done a thing over the year, plus he needed excitement. When young he was a good football player at UVA. They had little painted squares, the lime would cover it, for each ten-yard line. Laughing, talking, arguing about the beginning of baseball season, those men were in their element, a bunch of old jocks talking the talk.

"How's it look?" Harry called out.

"Straight. How does home plate look?"

"Solid. Tell you what, Moz made sure these lanes and the distance between them, the pitcher's mound, and home plate were exact. Exact. Not one inch over or under."

"Probably why he was such a winning coach." Susan stood up, and they heard her back crack. "Grandpa said Moz was one of the best coaches he'd ever seen. If times were different, Moz would have coached in the pros."

"Well, Susan, there's been some progress there, but hardly enough."

Susan looked. "Oh hey, here comes Taz."

The lovely architect joined them. "You know, we just might need to have a game once everything is dedicated."

"I'm for it. It's hot, but there's a breeze coming up. Feels better now than when we started." Susan, again on her hands and knees, looked up at Taz. "How's the front going?"

"Three weedwackers. Never would have thought so many people wanted to weedwack."

Harry laughed. "You don't see them back here with us."

"It looks easy. I would have thought you'd have a few hands. What is surprising to me are the bushes Windridge has given us. Baby crape myrtles, azaleas, extra boxwoods. Miranda is supervising the fall plants. Should be nice color here in the fall, plus good color next spring. She says when she and George ran the post office, they could hear the kids playing."

"George got the job once back from the war. She went to work with him. When I graduated from Smith, no idea what to do, she hired me. Of course, George was gone by then. But I still learned a lot." Harry loved Miranda. "Sometimes in good weather we'd walk over from the old post office and eat our lunch. The schools were always inviting, so quiet."

"Just watching her arrange plant groupings, I'm learning," Tazio agreed. "What the hell?" She stared at a dapper figure in Bermuda shorts striding toward them.

"Sandy." Susan, on her knees, made sure second base was perfectly sitting, not the least bit crooked.

"Hello, girls," he called.

They would have winced, but from Sandy, it seemed normal. He'd never get it, but he meant no harm.

"Hello. How do you like the front?"

"The plants? I'd hire Miranda to enhance any property. All she would need to do would be to see the site then make drawings."

"Well, you've seen her house," Harry affirmed his thoughts. "What do you think?"

"Back here?" The sound of the football fellows carried over and he glanced toward them. "It's so green. Tidy. What I like about behind the school is it's peaceful, feels country, but a big square would seem more civilized."

"Interesting." Tazio meant it. "Does anyone want a drink?"

"No, we've got a cooler at home plate," Harry replied.

"Where are your dogs and cats?" Sandy knew Harry usually came with her little family . . . well, Pirate wasn't so little.

"Home. I'm not laying down this chalk to have them traipse through it."

"You'll have to do it again just before Memorial Day," he said.

"Probably, but all I'll have to do is go over the lines. That's why I'm taking my time making sure I've got ninety feet between the bases."

"Don't forget the sixty feet, six inches to home plate from pitcher's mound," Sandy reminded her. "Course, you don't need chalk, but it needs to be mowed." He waved to Moz, then returned to the front of the schools.

"Moz will tell us what to do," Susan said. "Right now we are making certain of the distances, straight lines. It's taking longer than we thought, but we'll make sure it's perfect for the celebration. It really will be like old times for those who went to school here."

"I wonder." Tazio folded her arms across her chest.

"All of a sudden Sandy's showing up. Curiosity maybe." Susan brushed herself off. "Taz, I don't like this."

"I don't either," she agreed.

"It will be good to hear Jim out on Monday. You know he and Big Mim are discussing this. You called him and the first person he'd talk to is his wife." Harry swatted a fly with her baseball cap.

"Given that Mim's family owned half of Crozet since Monroe's time, she'll have clear opinions." Susan knew how closely her grandfather worked with Mim's people. "And the Sanburnes owned the other half." She laughed.

After Tazio walked to the front of the schools, Harry and Susan returned to their tasks. After forty-five minutes, they finished to their satisfaction.

"Let's ask Moz to look." Susan walked toward the roughly laid-out football field.

Moz and Armand came back with Susan.

"If I didn't know what year it was, I'd think we were ready for a big game." Moz grinned, clearly elated.

"We are. No reason why we can't have games after the dedication." Harry appreciated his praise.

"You know, Moz, that's not a bad idea. Keep the kids motivated," Armand said.

They all four walked up to the football field, then the two women left the men to their task, fueled by those ice-cold beers.

Turning to the front of the schools, they saw Sandy had already left there. Both women stopped, the sunlight shining on the big-paned windows, the grounds now setting off the buildings.

"I can't believe it." Harry's voice carried. "Miranda, it's beautiful. Beautiful."

"I've got a lot of help." She nodded toward Tazio; Paul, Tazio's husband; and a few of her gardening friends who were young. Young meaning in their sixties, for Miranda was in her eighties.

"This is so special." Susan's eyes watered a bit. "People have been so generous."

Tazio, all smiles, said, "People will be impressed and this really is a wonderful way to remember those who went before. Even in hard times there can be beauty."

As Harry and Susan turned toward Susan's station wagon, Sandy, returning, drove up.

"Come on, ladies, pile in. Short trip. I didn't go far. You, too, Taz."

"Have to go back to the office."

"This won't take fifteen minutes."

Harry shrugged. "Fifteen minutes. Okay, come on, Susan. But it better be good."

They hopped in. Susan up front, Harry in the back. "A new Lexus RX Hybrid."

"Bit the bullet. The Suburban was too big, had too many miles on it. I think I can fit clients in here."

"Plush." Susan admired the car. "Where are we going?"

"Spring Grove, right on the other side of Far Fields."

True to his word, they passed Far Fields in a few minutes. Harry noticed Arch Munson's truck.

The road, still unpaved, was wide. The lots, rectangular, two acres per, had most all the large trees intact. Each lot had some kind of pleasing prospect in it, facing west to the mountains; or if facing east, overlooking a long, low meadow with a meandering stream in it, trees scattered along the banks.

The lots had been thought out. Each building site could have even more privacy if the owner wished to plant more trees or hedges around the property borders.

The intended buyer would be solidly upper middle class.

"Arch and the boys."

Sandy looked to his left. "They do good work.

"Okay, nothing fully finished, but you get the idea." He pointed to the houses being built.

The old friends stared at two houses going up.

Harry noted, "One's half-done. The other has finishing work going on inside. The outside is lovely."

"There are seven lots in Spring Grove, from ten to thirty acres. The stone house should be done in six weeks. Took forever for the marble counters to come in."

"The only person I know who works in marble is Bunky Biche. Expensive." Harry leaned back in the comfortable seat.

"He's in there. There is a guy in Orange, another Italian, works around the clock," Sandy informed them. "The buyers want the best of everything."

"So they buy the lots, find their own contractor?" Susan gave anyone credit for the patience to build a house.

"We give buyers a list of who we think is the best, including interior decorators, landscapers, and architects."

"Sandy, why are we here?" Harry now leaned forward.

"I wanted you all to see a beautiful development. This would be what the school properties would look like. Top of the line. They would have to be Georgian or Federal."

"I remember." Susan did, too.

"They are impressive," Harry honestly said. "But I am opposed to a development there."

"I know that. But should I succeed, I want you to know it won't be tacky. No RVs in the driveways behind the house. No colored slides. Everything will be aesthetically controlled." His voice was firm. "Ready to go back?"

"Yes," Harry quickly said. "Sandy, you have wonderful ideas. I appreciate you taking us to Spring Grove."

Once back at the school, Sandy left.

"He's persistent," Susan noted. "The houses, the two we saw, are impressive. I'm sure what gets built on the other lots will be impressive, too. But no development here."

"I'm with you, girl. The whole committee is." Harry watched a milky butterfly visit a butterfly bush that Miranda had planted. "But doesn't it feel like this dropped out of the blue?"

"Does. I swear this is about more. The houses are probably only the beginning." Susan put her hands on her hips.

"I can't imagine what, but if there is more, I bet it means more money."

That phrase stuck with Harry while driving home. Fair was delivering a late foal, quite the surprise, so he wouldn't be there. She rang up Cooper, asking her to come over.

Once Cooper walked into the air-conditioned kitchen, Harry whipped out her cellphone to show Cooper the pictures of the new plantings, plus the back.

"Wow!"

"I hope that's what people say."

Pewter slept on the counter. Mrs. Murphy was curled in Harry's lap. The dogs, who had played outside in the heat, were sound asleep.

"While we're sitting here and I'm feeling so wonderful in this cool air, let me tell you, I found an odd bit of information, thanks to Denver's files in the basement at Mary Baldwin."

Harry interrupted, "In the basement? I mean they didn't throw stuff out?"

"I asked that question. His research and lectures were so unique, no one has been able to duplicate them. All the stuff about the Blue Ridge Mountains, the wildlife and human life moving ahead of the glaciers, he had files and files of the stuff. I asked them, wasn't there anyone else to teach this? The head of the Natural Sciences Department said people taught pieces of it. Her hope is that one day a student will take an interest and perhaps teach the course as a teaching assistant. Professor Raiselle took a broad approach; now it's all specialization. His notes make things understandable. A graduate student could understand it."

"I wonder if other universities keep papers."

"Of course they do, Harry. Why are they always building on to libraries? Think of Lafayette College. They have Lafayette's handwritten letters to General Washington. The mantra of any librarian is 'Never throw anything out.'"

Harry considered this. "It probably is useful for other people's research."

"Think of the Vatican Library."

Harry, whose mother was a librarian, wistfully said, "If Mom were alive, I would take her to Vatican City. I never had the chance to tell her or Dad how much I loved them and how much I learned from them. You don't start to understand what you did learn until your thirties. You know, Coop, people still come up to me who were students of Mom's to tell me how much she helped them when they needed to write papers. She always had time for people. I remember her reading the new books that came to the library. She loved her work."

"You never thought about it for yourself?" Cooper wondered.

"I need to be outdoors. I love to read, but at night. Anyway, what did you find? We got off track."

"We do that a lot." Cooper laughed. "He had invoices for work on the side. I checked his papers for the year he died, 2006. Nothing in conflict with teaching, but off jobs. When he was teaching, Roy Wheeler Realty was one of the big firms in Charlottesville. Still is, but in 2006 the real Roy Wheeler was running it. I know that because I called the company. Anyway, there was a bill for two hundred and seventy-one dollars, which seems modest, but for 1997 it was big enough. Raiselle studied, walked, and drilled for soil samples for the land on big estates that the company was representing for the sellers. Then I found other invoices for successful firms following Wheeler. There are so many realtors, high end, in Charlottesville, he probably could have made a living just serving them."

"What did they want to know?"

"The usual. Soil types, drainage, evidence for underground streams. Rocks underground and any rock formations overground, the hardest of rocks. Basic stuff," Cooper answered. "What if they wanted to put in a swimming pool or an infinity pool? Infinity pools were big then. If there was a lot of solid rock underneath . . . say, three feet of soil . . . that would be expensive. Plus, how much damage would you be doing to the stability of the house if you dug close to it? A rock seam might well be running under the house, and you'd be blowing up part of it, digging it with huge equipment. And if there was an underground stream, what would happen if you diverted it?"

"I would never have thought of any of that, and here I am with underground streams rolling through my farm. Well, yours, too."

"The first time I realized that was the year when it seemed to rain nonstop for three months. Pools appeared seemingly out of nowhere."

"And the creek stayed over its banks for months. I could hear it from the house," Harry remembered.

"Another thing I looked at," Cooper said, "easier for me to understand, was the correspondence with other professors, all over the world. An Argentine professor wrote him about the rocks under Bari's Loche. A rich place in his country. The focus from these people, a few women, was the pressure that had formed.

"I never thought of pressure. Now I look at the quartz in my soil and understand it forms as magma cools. I tried to think why he would be killed, so I poked around about geology.

"He even has a series of letters from a professor in Russia. The fellow wrote in English, but most of it was specialized geological vocabulary about quartz, shale, kyanite, and bluestone."

"We've got that stuff," Harry said. "I guess the shale vein is counties long. If something sparkles, I'll pick it up, but I don't know much other than a stone or crystal is pretty."

"One of the things about law enforcement, which I never would have thought about before I was in it, is how much you learn about murder victims or someone who died unexpectedly, say in a car crash. You find out their secrets. Oftentimes we find hidden bank accounts. People selling contraband, and it's not always booze or drugs. High-end antiques can be contraband. I think we often know the dead better than those who knew them while living."

"Can you think of anything illegal with rock formations?"

"No. That isn't to say that Denver Raiselle wasn't involved in something. Nothing pops up. He may well be a fellow who crossed a nutcase, or maybe he put the moves on another man's wife. Nothing has appeared that drives me to a conclusion of illegal activity, but people don't get shot for nothing."

"No. You're making me think about what's underground." Harry took a deep breath. "Can you find the type of radar that people use to uncover treasure or buried bodies, old tombs?"

Cooper's eyes widened. "It's used, depending on the case. Archaeologists use it all the time. What are you thinking about?"

"I want to go over the land behind the schoolhouse."

"Well . . ." Cooper paused for a long time. "It is possible you might find buried bodies. There's no way to know. As for geological formations, that I also don't know, but I can't see it would be important."

"I'm thinking ahead. This money offer truly disturbs me. I'm in a fog. So I want to make a preemptive strike. If you, Susan, Taz, and I go back there and cover all those acres, should we find . . . say, graves, crystals, enslaved or native people . . . that complicates a sale."

Cooper's eyes narrowed; she breathed a deep breath. "Harry, you're right. Can you do this without anyone finding out?"

"I don't know."

"I think you're on to something. Let me sniff around."

"I'm not telling anyone until you know. Not even Susan."

"Right. Better safe than sorry." The minute that was out of her mouth, Cooper wished she hadn't said it, as the murkiness of events did not lead themselves to safety.

16

May 19, 2024

Sunday

Wearing a tool belt tied around her waist, Harry walked alongside Ned, who was sweeping his metal detector. Three other people also walked the back acres of the schools.

Paul, Tazio's husband, swung his detector back and forth; Tazio walked with him. She, too, wore a tool belt. Cooper used a detector, Susan walking with her. A small pile of spades rested in the middle of the field. All were careful not to disturb the carefully placed, straight chalk lines for the baseball diamond and the football field, which was still half-finished.

"Here." Ned stopped.

Harry knelt down, took her small gardening hand tool out of her belt, and dug. "Got it."

She pulled up two old pennies, placing them in the other pocket on her tool belt.

The six people, with weather quite pleasant, covered the entire field in three hours. They could have speeded up, but by going slow, they felt, they wouldn't miss anything.

Tucker and Pirate walked with Harry. Pirate could smell whatever Harry dropped in her belt.

"Anything good?" Tucker asked.

"Coins." Pirate had learned a lot about coins as a puppy, when he'd knocked over Harry's big jar of pennies, dimes, and nickels.

Finally finished, the group carried their tools to the front of the schools. Ned had brought a table, which he'd set up before they started their task.

Susan opened the back of the station wagon, pulling out a red-checkered tablecloth, which she placed over the table.

"Susan." Tazio smiled.

"Ever so proper." Harry teased her best friend.

Out came the coolers, one with drinks, one with sandwiches. The men set up the folding chairs. Mrs. Murphy and Pewter, patrolling the schools from the outside, joined them. The cats knew ways to get into the buildings, which the people did not. Pewter was exceptionally talented at opening doors lacking double locks. As it was, there were a few signs of mice, but mostly they had the place to themselves. Mouse patrol was an important job.

Paul brought a smaller table out of his truck. For work, he trained Big Mim's Thoroughbreds. Like many animal people, he wasn't much of a talker, so when he did open his mouth, his friends listened.

He patted the table. "You can put your finds here after we eat."

"Good idea." Harry, famished, devoured half of an egg salad sandwich.

"I made those for you." Susan took one herself.

"I can't resist egg salad. You make the best. Best deviled eggs, too."

Paul surprised everyone. "Have you tried my wife's? You should."

"Now, honey." Tazio glowed.

"Everyone has their specialty." Cooper found all that walking had tired her a bit. "Harry's is shepherd's pie. On a cold, cold day, you want to be at her table."

"That's the truth." Fair nodded. "And I will go on record saying my T-bone steak cooked on the grill is pretty terrific."

"He's right." Pewter loved those tidbits.

"Oh, Fair, your grill is better than most people's kitchen stoves. I remember when you bought that thing," Ned, himself a competitive griller, announced.

"I do, too." Harry laughed.

"I had to give my bride smelling salts." Fair laughed.

They compared recipes, favorite foods, the lack of an outstanding restaurant in Crozet. Oh, there were a couple of places where one could grab a sandwich, but there wasn't a terrific restaurant.

"Everyone drives to Charlottesville," Tazio said. "Finding parking makes this less than desirable."

"Parking at Burton's is good." Harry mentioned a favorite at Stonefield Shopping Center.

"Actually, there's a couple of downtown restaurants, like the Black Cow, which are outstanding. Parking's not so good though." Still, Ned went, as he liked to eat out.

Susan, not so much, but she went along. Made him happy.

Cooper, who had inhaled her food, got up, walked over to the treasure table. "Okay, until the brownies and cookies come out, I'll tell you what we found. Then I'll sit down."

"Well, another belt buckle," Harry called out. "There really may be soldiers out there."

"What a help that would be." Susan reached for another egg sandwich just as Harry did.

"Lots of coins." Cooper put some in her palm, swirled them around to get a little of the dirt off. "A great deal from the 1920s, and here are a few from the 1970s, which is funny. They're old. Lots more from the forties, solid steel pennies, and a few from the fifties. People lose coins. You have a hole in your pants pocket, and out they fall. Or you drop one."

"Anything else?"

"Couple of nails. Anything we found was close to the surface. The metal detectors, I find, are the best finding items from close to the surface to sixteen inches. In theory, the machines are supposed to register metal even deeper, but the soil has to be just right for that. These things can detect large metal objects, too. If an iron box were down there, say two feet, we'd see it register. Still, this is useful."

"Will it help if you get Rick to bring out the Ground Penetrating Radar machine?" Harry felt hopeful.

"If you give me a clear outline . . . you know, what we have, why we need to know more . . . I think he will."

"Coop, what does the radar show?"

"It can show metal buried deeper, but it's especially good for rock formations, determining underground water, soil types, all of which affects the value of the land. It's used by the electric company to mark underground lines so you don't dig them up if you're digging around your home. Cut one of those lines and you're out of luck until a crew can come out to fix such a small problem."

"How do you know all this?" Tazio smiled at Cooper.

"After Harry and I talked, I did some research. Also talked to officers from northern Virginia who use it frequently. More people. More need. Anyway, it works. Here's where it can be dicey: If you have clay soil, it's highly conductive, so that slows or inhibits penetration depth. Chances are, there might be a clay soil seam underneath back there. It's not on the surface, but also certain kinds of rocks can absorb GPR signals. That's why if Rick gives me the go-ahead, I have to use a trained officer to do this. None of us could just walk behind what looks like an old lawn mower. Has to be a trained technician." Cooper took a breath. "It's possible there are old bodies buried. It's also possible there are streams running underground to Swift Creek, good soils perhaps. Who knows?"

"We see Jim Sanburne tomorrow." Ned looked at his wife, who nodded affirmation. "He'll go for it."

"Out of curiosity, what would it cost to rent one?" Tazio asked.

"Depending on the size of the machine, you'd start at a thousand dollars per day, plus the cost of the operator. The equipment your utility company uses, some of those detectors cost upwards of a hundred thousand dollars, a great deal, but think of the money they save. Cutting a major electric line is a disaster," Cooper answered. "What law enforcement uses varies with the job. Do some departments have access to large equipment? They do. Some own their own equipment, usually not as powerful as the utility company models, but if there's a recent missing person, eventually the radar detectors will come out."

The others remained silent for a moment.

"Well, I think we've been successful. We found enough objects to justify further exploration. Most of you know I found a partly squashed Union belt buckle back here. In the creek sand," Harry said.

Sandy Rycroft drove up, stopped, got out. "Looks like a picnic."

Tazio, polite, invited him. "Sit down. There's food left."

"Thank you, but no. I saw the cars, trucks, and then the picnic. My curiosity got the better of me."

"As in, what are we doing?" Harry pointed to a brownie.

It looked too good. Sandy picked it up. "Well . . ."

"Soon." Susan laughed. "What else are you curious about?"

"The land, obviously."

"I found an old Union belt buckle, quartz. So I began to wonder what's really out there."

"Me too," he agreed. "My father had an interest in the schools. That was so long ago, though, plus it was easier to develop in other areas."

"Anything is possible. We've concentrated on the buildings, not the land." Ned sounded more fearful than he intended to sound.

"Harry, you mentioned an old Union belt buckle." Sandy raised his eyebrows.

"Found it in the creek. Maybe there are soldiers buried out there." She gestured toward the back acres.

Immediately, Sandy promised, "If there are, we would protect them, put up a marker. My partners would be very respectful."

A silence followed this.

Tazio, as the leader, spoke. "I have no doubt you would be respectful, but we aren't going to support a sale."

He brushed his hands together to remove the brownie crumbs. "I can see that. Well, I didn't mean to crash the party."

He thanked them again, got back in his car, and drove off.

"All right, let's clean up." Harry started lifting paper plates. "I'll give him credit for persistence."

"If we do find evidence with a GPR, it can complicate things for all of us, especially if someone wants to make trouble. Complicates it more for developers, obviously." Tazio grabbed a sandwich to take home.

"Hard to battle history," Harry agreed.

Ned, having seen so much, thanks to his career, softly replied, "You'd be surprised."

17

May 20, 2024

Monday

The coins, uniform buttons, a broken chain possibly to a pocket watch, all had been cleaned, polished. The finds from the metal detectors filled a breakfast bowl.

Jim Sanburne rooted around the bowl, fascinated by the finds.

The restoration committee sat in his office, which was exactly the same as it had been for decades. The chairs faced Jim as he placed his office chair in their circle, a coffee table in the middle. No one could accuse Crozet of spending money on a fancy office. His small office had heat as well as air-conditioning, which was all he needed. Good lighting helped. The older Jim became, the less he wanted his surroundings changed.

"This is one day's work?" He pushed a penny, not shiny, from 1902. More recent pennies, such as those from the 1930s, could be shined up, but the 1902 one was too old.

"It is," Tazio answered. "We could find more, but we thought to come to you with what turned up with simple metal detectors."

"If we had Ground Penetrating Radar, we'd find much more," Harry eagerly suggested.

"I can see that."

Ned, who had joined them, gave Jim the background with Hickory Real Estate and Sandy Rycroft.

"Hmm," he murmured. "Sandy's a good businessman. We know the school property now has more value."

"Law enforcement uses GPR a lot. The machine is expensive to rent for a regular citizen," Susan chimed in. "But we'd like to have more information, especially since we are unsure of what Sandy might do."

Jim picked up a uniform button. "Certainly looks like a button off a Federal uniform. Indiana." He shifted in his seat. "I'll call Rick. I'll mention there may be bodies. If there are and any of them are soldiers from the Civil War, I would think it would be easier in getting a historical plaque for the school and grounds . . . once all is proven, of course."

"Yes, it would. Proving who is under there, if there are people laid to rest, shouldn't be that time-consuming. We'd know right away if they are male or female. DNA can fill in the rest, and bones provide that. Naturally, one can't casually disturb such remains." Ned folded his hands together. "We would also know more about soils, stuff like that. It could be helpful in protecting the place. It's very obvious that Sandy is serious."

Harry added, "My belt buckle was from an Indian regiment. Maybe there are more men out there."

Jim smiled. "I'll push for the GPR tomorrow."

They all thanked him at once.

Fair knocked on the door and came in. "Sorry I'm late."

Jim, who liked Fair as a man and as a vet, motioned for him to pull up a chair. "You've missed out on the comfortable seats. We were just discussing a history plaque for the schools, among other things, which will naturally mention that I am the mayor." He laughed. "Maybe we can slot in my wife."

No one knew whether he was serious or not; Jim was a teaser.

"You know, we could dedicate a building to her, provided she helps find original items for the interiors. I'm only thinking out loud." Tazio liked the game.

"No, build a barn in her name. You know that they had horses and one old wagon before cars." Harry had been researching the school for years. "Given the relative poverty of the students there, wasn't much by way of material things. And what they had was usually a decade behind the materials at white schools. Sometimes more. If a teacher was accustomed to, say, a woodburning stove, despite electricity, then a woodburning stove was used. Electricity proved expensive, regardless of decade, and a teacher who saved expenses also saved their job."

"You all speak softly for a minute." Jim dialed his phone. "Rick, glad to catch you." Pause. "No, everything is good here. No accidents, no protests. It's finally spring. Still cool, but spring. Listen, can you get two GPR machines to the schools by tomorrow? The committee has used a metal detector and found some items that suggest there may be unusual soils there, and maybe even the bodies of soldiers." Jim put his hand over the mouthpiece of the phone, made the okay sign. "Thanks, Rick. If there is anything unusual, it might make the news. Good for Crozet." Pause. "Okay. Thanks again." He hung up the phone. "He'll have two GPRs there tomorrow at nine. Cover the entire twenty acres."

Susan jumped up, then sat back down. "Sorry. It's just I'm so excited."

"I wasn't joking about the news. This is made for Memorial Day. Especially if there are buried soldiers. People who fought for others, for freedom. And it gives us a chance to tell what Walter Plecker really did. Do you have a tribal speaker?"

"We have Norton Sessions, who is Cherokee," Tazio supplied. "We have a good group of speakers."

Jim smiled. "You all have been busy putting everything together."

"Yes. It's one of the things the Bureau of Indian Affairs unfortunately used to avoid recognizing tribes. So many Native Americans had intermarried with white people, Black people, and those of other tribes. Norman will do a good job. They couldn't accurately fill out those hideous papers to prove who they were, their blood," Tazio replied. "The Feds wanted documents from people who had been pushed into being identified as mixed race."

Jim leaned back in his chair. "Can any of us prove our blood? I'm willing to bet there are very few of us who can go back in time on both sides of our parents' families."

Susan responded, "Harry and I were with Cooper to clean up the Jones graveyard. They can go way back. But again, how many people can you identify on both sides of the family? Short memories. Time keeps moving forward."

"That may be a good thing." Jim smiled.

They left the office, giving more thanks and hugs. As it was late afternoon, everyone needed to get back to work, but they wanted a moment to share their excitement and relief that this was happening fast.

Tazio lifted her hands up like a football captain celebrating. "To tomorrow."

"Tomorrow," they cheered.

18

May 21, 2024

Tuesday

Harry watched two men using Ground Penetrating Radar. It looked easy enough as they walked behind the equipment somewhat resembling a push lawn mower. Susan and Lucas joined her, but Ned, Fair, and Tazio had to work. There was no point in sitting in lawn chairs watching the men, so the three unlocked the school gym.

"Clean." Lucas was impressed. "Who polished the floor?"

"I did." Harry looked down at Mrs. Murphy, Pewter, Tucker, and Pirate. "I had help. Those furry paws shine the wood."

"Finally. Some credit." Pewter appeared self-satisfied.

The other three followed the humans as they walked to the wall.

"The idea is to put up the large wooden plaques with students' names on them, here." Susan pointed to the long walls. "Ned found a sign painter in Richmond who gave us a good price. Over here we'll put up the plaques with teachers' names, starting with Miss Letitia Small. All those teachers performed miracles."

"Everyone's name?" Lucas was astonished. "How did you find the roll call?"

"My wonderful husband dug out the school records, down in Richmond. He copied everything, said it's amazing what's there. Mostly no one knows or cares, but if someone is researching, say, the beginnings of Western Albemarle High School or the Governor's Schools, everything is there. There was a time when things were put on microfilm to save space, but Virginia still kept the original records in some cases, because of who was involved. Our early leaders were interested in education. Jefferson, obviously, but also other public servants, governors, felt strongly that the only hope for our nation was educated citizens. We take reading and writing for granted. They did not." Susan had heard from the time she was little that she had to get a good education, and she did.

"Can you imagine holding a letter written by James Madison or Monroe?" Lucas was also fond of history.

"Once slavery was outlawed, that first free generation started reading and writing, which was a breakthrough. Mostly, people needed work that paid, but a few souls used reading and writing to unearth their history as best they could. This state is rich in history and the people dedicated to it. Ned also said the uproar over the women's vote bounced up all manner of speeches in our General Assembly." Susan, back to the plaques, pointed to the top of the ceiling. "If we placed the plaques there, it's too high. No one could read a thing. What about if we place them, say, at eye level for a six-footer? A short person will still be able to read it. We're going to fill this wall and the other one."

"What if we start, and find out if we have to double up? Put one on top of another?" Harry wasn't sure about this.

"Well . . ." Susan pondered.

"There will be other spaces. If worse comes to worst, why can't we start here, and what's left over will be put in the schools?" Lucas suggested.

"We've had that fight." Harry smiled.

"Except for Harry and myself, the committee wants the school walls to have the children's drawings, and also what was on the walls when they studied," Susan filled him in.

"Like photographs of whoever was president," Harry added.

"Oh, I see, as though those kids are still studying. That does sound more involved," Lucas agreed.

"We even have some of the teachers' attendance books, coursework. No one cared. When we started, this building was jammed with old trunks, tools, mops, stuff like that. The trunks had teachers' belongings. I was amazed. The teachers were tough. If someone missed class, they had to stay late or get docked. No wiggle room." Harry admired those teachers.

"I asked my grandmother about the teachers. She knew them from when she married Grandad and moved here. She said they were hard on the kids, and her explanation is that it's because life was stacked against them, employment, stuff like that. And she said those teachers were adamant that the students vote once they turned twenty-one. I believe those youngsters were better prepared than our students today. I really do."

"I sometimes think what we have now is babysitting. Also, the teachers get no support. Not like the days when parents backed up teachers' decisions. Everyone focuses on the bad behavior of the students, but I think they've been abandoned. How can you learn if you aren't held to a standard?" Harry, like Susan, cared about education.

"I don't know," Lucas quietly replied. "Teaching and school libraries have been so politicized. It's a wonder anyone can learn anything."

"Well, doesn't a good teacher make you want to learn?" Harry fired back.

Susan tapped Lucas's forearm. "She's tough duty, I agree. You've got one chance to learn with your generation. Sure, you can learn in your thirties and beyond, but it's not the same. That's one of the things that got me so interested in these schools, once Tazio brought them to my attention. Those youngsters had one chance. They were kept from the white kids, but they still had teachers who cared. Have you seen the schoolbooks?"

"You showed them to me when I first moved here," Lucas replied.

"So I did. My memory can be spotty," Susan confessed.

Lucas, ever a gentleman, said, "If I had as much to remember as you do, I'd let a few things slip, too. I nearly went crazy reading all the bills floating in the House of Delegates. Had to make notes. Still have to make notes; fortunately I don't need copious notes to cut hay."

"I often think life is one great curveball." Harry sighed. "Sometimes you can hit it and sometimes you can't. Okay, back to the names."

"The best way is to measure these long walls, and when we get the painted plaques, measure them, too. That ought to tell us if we'll have some left over, and also if we have to double up. I don't know how we can double up and expect people to see though."

"Someone's coming," Tucker barked.

The GPR operators, two men, young, stuck their heads in the open doorway.

"Come on in," Susan invited them.

"We've got something. You might want to have a look," Gerard, the taller fellow, told them.

The three looked at one another, following the two operators outside. The animals followed, too.

Oliver, the shorter fellow, curly black hair, walked them to the back of the baseball diamond, center field. He turned on his GPR, rolled it over a spot.

The dial registered the depth of the electromagnetic impulses.

Oliver stopped. "Eight feet."

"Good Lord," Susan exclaimed.

Lucas and Harry said nothing, but stared at what appeared to be a family grouping. The long-dead bodies, skeletons only, were arranged next to one another, heads pointing east.

"They were probably Christians," Harry quietly said. "Christians are, at least they were in the old days, buried facing the sunrise, for hope."

"Do you know who owned this land?" Lucas wondered.

"Yes, the Coleman family." Susan kept staring. "I doubt this contains any of their remains. They are buried in the big cemetery on Crozet Road."

"We'll mark this." Gerard had done a lot of law enforcement work.

"Anything else?" Susan asked.

"There is a seam of soil or slate that absorbs our signals. The radar doesn't penetrate beyond the seam. It's possible there's something under that. Clay is difficult to dig and no one would attempt to go through slate." Gerard turned on his machine. "Around here, it's almost always clay but the slate seam . . . the edges of it might reach here . . . it runs through counties. We'll keep going. It's possible there's more."

Lucas asked, "How accurate is the GPR in finding graves?"

"Very accurate. That's why we're used so much by cops." Oliver turned on his machine again. "These are old bodies. Bones. But if, say, it's a recent murder victim. We get it. Next time you see a Central Virginia Electric Cooperative guy running over your lawn, painting where lines are buried, think of this. There's a lot we can see. It saves money. Knowing what's underground helps. No one wants to dig granite."

"No," Lucas agreed.

"All right, you two keep going. I'll make a few calls." Susan let them get back to work.

The three walked to the gym, then continued to Susan's car. She opened the door, sat in the driver's seat, and pulled out her cellphone. "I'll call Jim first, then Tazio."

She got Jim right away, gave him the news, clicked off, and called Tazio, who was thrilled.

Turning off her phone, Susan looked up at her two friends. "Well, this is something."

"What do we do now?" Harry put her hand on Pirate's head.

"Nothing. Wait. See what else turns up, then we need to meet as a group. Oh, by the way, Jim was funny. He said, 'Wait until Sandy Rycroft hears this.' "

They returned to the gym. An hour later, the two men again called to them.

"More bodies?"

There were seven more bodies, again facing east.

"Whoever they were, someone took great care to bury them properly," Harry remarked.

"Pretty much rules out unintended death, I would think." Susan thanked the two men. "I'll wait to call Jim and Tazio until you're finished."

"We'll be another hour. We go slow." Gerard turned his machine back on, started walking. "Also, we keep hitting that seam. Can't penetrate it."

"Did you notice if the bodies up here had belt buckles?" Lucas asked.

"I did," Harry replied, then added, "I'm being a wuss, but seeing those skeletons with U.S. buckles gave me the creeps. Brought me back to the skeleton we pulled out of the water."

Lucas nodded. "Me too."

"Why do people not like human bones?" Pirate asked.

"They aren't supposed to disturb the dead," Tucker told him. *"But bones aren't as bad as fresh dead people. Humans don't like that."*

19

May 22, 2024

Wednesday

Sandy Rycroft had heard about the GPR. He was on the phone. "All it means is we can't tear up those acres."

"But eventually we will need to do that. When this goes through . . . and Sandy, you know our partners, it has to go through . . . everything back there will be dug up."

Sandy replied, "We should give this a year."

A pause followed. "Get the deal done. No texts. I'm throwing out the cell."

"You always do that."

"Yes. No one must know we are working together. Now get on it."

The phone clicked off. Sandy took a deep breath, his heart racing.

Tazio remarked as Lucas, Fair, Susan, and Ned were working in her office, "Let's not disturb the dead. We don't need to do that right now. Later we can see if the dead can be identified."

Lucas said, "It's possible some of the people whose children studied here were so poor, they couldn't afford to be buried in a cemetery. The soldiers, again, were the prisoners of war. Maybe not the first thing you would think of, but the family could be anyone. But whoever they were, they received no markers, no memories."

"Or no one could afford a marker," Fair said.

Susan got up. "I'm calling Moz and Sherry."

"They usually have the right idea." Ned smiled.

"Moz, how are you?" Pause. "I have a question. Were there families so poor that they had no place to be buried? I'm wondering if anyone from the school is buried in the back," Susan said.

"Not that I know about, or at least not while I was there," the burly coach answered. "There was talk of possible Federal soldiers being buried. I don't know if they were stationed here. Never heard that. Could have been shot when moving through, or captured. There wasn't much looking back."

"We used Ground Penetrating Radar yesterday, thanks to Sheriff Shaw, and found what appears to be a family, and then some other bodies. The Union buckle's obvious. None of this is public yet. There's no reason for that, especially before the dedication."

"What provoked this?" Moz motioned for Sherry to come close to listen.

"Sandy Rycroft wants to buy us off, the restoration committee, and he offered a high amount for the land. A development behind the schools, around the fields, would make a lot of money."

"Buy you off?"

"He offered us each a hundred and fifty thousand dollars, plus millions for Crozet."

Sherry, having heard that, butted in. "To build houses?"

"That's what he said. They'd build houses around the land, kind of like a park. The land would be shared by the homeowners. The five acres behind the schools would stay with the schools."

"You can't trust that," Sherry quickly responded. "Not just Sandy, but any real estate firm that wants to build a development."

"I'm with her," Moz added, sharing the mouthpiece.

"Jim Sanburne said he wouldn't agree to such a thing." Susan took a glass of champagne offered by Ned. "It's too complicated, too divisive."

"Jim is right. A lot of people in town will get in an uproar. There will be those who think the town could use the money, which it does. But others, who don't want a development and more traffic, would fight back. This will cause so much trouble."

Listening to Moz, Susan agreed, then promised him, "I'll keep you posted. We're trying to figure out what to do about the bodies."

Moz firmly advised her, "Let those who are asleep stay asleep."

They signed off. Susan relayed Moz and Sherry's thoughts to the others.

"It's possible there are soldiers there. But the other bodies, also skeletons, varying in size, I'd bet that's a family." Lucas, like Ned, was wondering if there might be any records in the State Capitol. There were none in Crozet.

Tazio leaned forward in her chair. "We need to ignore this. In the future, can the fact that bodies are back there slow down or put off Sandy Rycroft—and whoever his investors are?"

A long silence followed.

Finally, Fair set down his glass. "You have a point, Tazio."

Lucas agreed. "If we don't do this, we look irresponsible. No matter who is down there, there is bound to be a group that wishes to create some memorial."

"I guess." Susan waffled. "But I'd prefer if we can just sit on this for now."

While the group talked, Sandy Rycroft paid a visit to Jim Sanburne.

"I've heard the current scuttlebutt."

"Yes." Jim sat in a comfortable chair. "People notice equipment like GPR machines, trucks at the school, but how did you find out the details?"

"I can't reveal my sources. We will not desecrate the deceased."

"I would hope not. Besides, you have to buy the land first, Sandy. You're putting the cart before the horse. You know I am opposed to this."

"I do, but Jim, you'll come out ahead, regardless of what happens." Sandy smiled.

"I don't know about that, but I do know you'll make a fortune."

Sandy blinked. "Yes, I'll be well rewarded. My father counseled me when young not to be greedy. I think I'm being reasonable. He also counseled me not to become a Russian professor. I'm glad I didn't. I make good money, but I'm not destructive to the beauty of the land here."

"I know." Jim knew a great deal of money was at stake, but he was thinking perhaps there was more than he'd realized. If push came to shove, Hickory Real Estate and its partners could find land closer, but not as close. Sandy was so eager, Jim pondered what he was missing.

He looked out his window, to see Sandy walk to his car as Armand was walking to his big SUV from the opposite direction.

The two men stood for a moment, Sandy talking, Armand listening. Armand looked surprised to be addressed, but he nodded kindly all the same.

Armand patted Sandy on the back, which somewhat soothed the realtor. Then he got in his car and drove away.

Jim could see how upset Sandy was. No pat on the back could fix that. He wondered what this possible find and potential delay might mean financially.

20

May 23, 2024

Thursday

Harry looked at her chore list. This would be a long day.

"Oh hell." She walked past the kitchen table and saw one of Fair's file folders on it.

No point calling him. She might as well run it to the clinic. The big old clock with the numbers in Roman numerals registered 8:11. She liked clocks, especially when they told the correct time. Throwing on a light sweater to ward off the late-spring chill, she called to her pets.

"*I'm coming.*" Tucker lifted her head, hurrying from the living room to the kitchen.

Pirate, flat out on the screened-in porch, rose, but it took him longer. There was a lot to get up.

Mrs. Murphy and Pewter heard her, but they were already outside, under the walnut tree. They sat and waited to see which vehicle Harry would take. After she closed the house door behind her, then the screen door, she crossed the neatly mowed front yard.

"Make up your mind," Pewter fussed as Harry considered the old Ford F-150 or the not-as-old Volvo.

"All right." She opened the back of the station wagon, Pirate jumped in. She kept the backseat down, which meant everyone could be together. It was easier for the Irish Wolfhound to jump in from the rear. Pewter and Mrs. Murphy sat on the folder, which Harry had placed on the passenger seat. Why waste time with dogs?

"I wouldn't mind a drive." Pewter liked looking out the window as Harry drove toward town.

Harry turned on the radio; she liked the classical station.

About fifteen minutes later, crossing under the railroad tracks—the overhead pass was an easy site to use for directions—she turned right at the light.

"Are we going the back way?" Pirate had learned the roads.

"She probably wants to see what's blooming at the orchard," Mrs. Murphy told him. *"The peaches were early. The apples are a bit late. She loves the blooms."*

"I'm curious. One short stop." Harry turned onto the road to the schools.

Once there, she stopped and let out the dogs and cats, then walked around the back of the buildings. Arms across her chest, she stared at the lovely green expanse, now marked for the football game as well as baseball.

"Hmm." Tucker lifted her nose.

"Blood." Pirate also raised his head.

"You know, kids, I bet there are long-ago bodies under houses in town. Who knows, maybe even at the fire department. There have been people here since it was called Wayland's Crossing. Maybe we'll never know how long some of the tribes lived here."

Tucker trotted toward the gym, followed by the others. Harry watched, then walked farther down the twenty-acre quad. The creek chugged along. They'd had rain off and on. The sound was soothing.

Tucker's bark was not. *"Mom."*

"Bother." Harry ignored her. Rabbits, deer, possum, gophers all lived around the place.

"Mom," Tucker barked.

"She needs encouragement," Mrs. Murphy counseled.

Tucker, accompanied by Pirate, came from around the back of the gym building, racing toward Harry.

"Come on. It's important."

Harry looked at her corgi. "Calm down."

Pirate stood close, nudging her.

Still no response, so Tucker grabbed Harry's jeans, pulling on the fabric.

"Tucker."

"Come on." She kept pulling, even stepping on Harry's sneaker, while Pirate headbutted Harry from behind.

"What's got into you two?"

Neither barked. They kept moving their human toward the gym, which was perhaps an acre away. Finally Harry walked where they were leading her. She figured something had them in a twit, because the cats weren't with them. Maybe the cats had gotten into trouble. She picked up her pace.

As Harry rounded the gym building, Tucker let go of her leg, leaving tooth marks in the jeans. She saw Sandy Rycroft on his back, the cats sitting with him. Running to him, she knelt down.

Glassy-eyed but breathing, he lifted his hand . . . a deep slash was across his palm . . . then she noticed the blood on the front of his shirt, some on his jacket. He moved his lips, but no sound emerged.

"Sandy. Sandy. Hold tight. I'll call 911." Luckily she had her cell in her hip pocket. She dialed 911.

"Hello, it's Harry Haristeen, I'm at the schools. I'm with a badly injured person. He's been stabbed." She listened. "Okay." Then she looked down at Sandy. "They're on their way. They're close, Sandy. Hang on."

His eyes fluttered. His muscles twitched. He gurgled. His eyes stopped moving.

Harry immediately began pumping his chest. Avoiding the wound, or where she thought it was, as blood kept oozing out of him—pump and pump, then stop and breathe into his mouth.

"Dear God, please save him."

The ambulance crew was quick, since their building was just on the north side of the railroad tracks. She heard the siren. Then she heard a second one, farther away. The ambulance was at the gym in ten minutes' time. Meanwhile, she kept on trying to revive Sandy. Two paramedics ran to her.

Howard Finster took over. Harry said nothing. The animals watched as the other emergency volunteer hurried up to them. She helped as best she could. But clearly, Sandy was gone.

The other sirens drew closer. Cut off. Harry heard footsteps running. Cooper now knelt down by Sandy. She took his pulse. Then carefully dropped his arm.

"Did you see anyone?"

Harry replied, "No."

"How long have you been here?"

"Maybe twenty minutes. I just found him."

Cooper stood up, looking around. "Everyone stay. I'll call Rick. If we get forensics here right away, we might find something. You all can move the body as soon as they're done. Harry, tell me exactly what happened. How did you find him?"

"I was out back, looking over the baseball diamond and the football field. Tucker kept barking. I ignored her. She and Pirate came to me. Tucker pulled on my pants' leg. I followed the dogs and found Sandy. He was alive. He tried to speak but couldn't. I called emergency. By the time I told them where we were, I saw he was dying. I tried to resuscitate him. I saw no cars. Nothing."

Cooper looked at the dead man. "He fought. His hand is deeply sliced. Do you know if he had enemies? You knew him better and longer than I did."

"I can't think of anyone. He seemed to work well with other people. I never heard bad talk about him, nor did I ever hear he had cheated a client. No tales of him cheating on his wife either, speaking of cheating. He wasn't aggressive. That's the only way I can think to describe him. You know, the kind of guy that might call you once a week to check in if you were doing business with him. Hickory Real Estate is successful. As I never sold or bought anything, I'm not the best reference though."

"You're helpful." Cooper looked at Sandy again. "A painful way to die. Whoever killed him was close."

Harry nodded her head in agreement. "Yesterday old bones. Today murder."

"Go home. I'll take a statement later. The fewer people here, the better. Maybe we'll find something . . . a bit of paper, a key, I don't know. He struggled."

Harry took the animals to the station wagon. They got in just as forensics pulled up, followed by Sheriff Shaw.

She held up her hand to them as she drove out.

"Fresh blood. Strong," Pirate remarked.

"She can't smell it." Tucker hoped humans could smell a little something, as fresh blood is very distinctive.

"You know, I need to get ahold of myself. I'll call Fair, then Susan, when I get home. I need a cup of tea or something. I wasn't Sandy's biggest fan. I wasn't happy about the offer for the land, but I certainly didn't want him dead." She gulped air. "This started out as a late spring, not much going on. Then we pulled up a body from Swift Creek. Yesterday, bodies were found under the ground back there. And now a murder. What in the hell is going on?"

"Best to keep your nose out of it." Mrs. Murphy offered sage advice.

Fair, having taken off work, walked through the back door forty-five minutes later. He found his wife sitting at the kitchen table, staring into space. She had a notebook by her, pen in hand. The dogs rested at her feet. The cats sat on the table.

She looked up. "Hi, honey."

He walked behind her, putting his arms around her, kissing her on the cheek. "I'm sorry you had such an awful morning."

"You know . . ." She paused. "It was."

He sat down, the dogs bestirred themselves to come over for head pets. The cats merely opened one eye.

"Can I get you something?"

"No," she replied. "I was looking out the window. Trying to empty my mind. Made me feel better." She took a deep breath. "He was alive when I found him . . . barely, but still alive. His eyes were open. He was breathing. I don't know if he knew it was me. I immediately called the emergency number. He died while I was on the phone. A flutter, a couple of spasms."

"I'm sorry, honey. Are you sure I can't get you something? Maybe a drink with a punch?"

"No."

"I was with Mom when she died. It's not the same, but there is that moment when they're gone. You feel it. Sandy had a lot of life left. Why would anyone want to kill him?" Fair wondered.

"I can't get that out of my head. Or the blood."

"You must have arrived close to the time he was killed. Thank God no one came after you."

"I thought of that, but there was no car, no bicycle. I would have seen either. You name it. Just Sandy collapsed behind the gym. So I missed the killer by maybe fifteen minutes, plus I would have heard a car. There's only one way in and out."

"Honey, let me get you something. Please. Just a sip, or perhaps aspirin."

"I don't have any pain, but I guess I'll drink a hot tea. You didn't have to come home. I'm okay. Stunned, but okay."

"You've suffered a terrible jolt. It's one thing to pull up a car with old bones. Gruesome, surprising, but this . . . this. My God, what if you had walked in on the killing?"

As he moved to the stove, Tucker boldly pronounced, "*I would have protected you, Mom.*"

"*Me too,*" the gentle giant echoed.

"*Oh, you could have bitten ankles. I could have scratched the killer's eyes out. Blinded him.*" Pewter puffed her chest.

Mrs. Murphy remained silent.

"While you're up, how about some Temptations treats for the cats and a Greenie each for the dogs? The dogs took me to Sandy. The cats were waiting there."

"Sure." He opened the cabinet doors, such a pleasing sound, and suddenly he had four animals right next to him. Everyone got a treat.

"I've gone over and over in my mind what could propel anyone to kill Sandy Rycroft. And why was he at the schools?"

"Maybe he came to look again. He wanted that land."

"But he didn't come in his car. That tells me he was driven there. See what I mean? I can't stop turning stuff over in my head. This was deliberate. He was driven there."

"That makes sense. It's possible he walked there if he trusted his killer, but someone would have noticed. Rick will find that stuff out, but you are right, the schools were the destination." He put hot tea in front of her and a croissant, just in case.

Harry almost always had a croissant or biscuit in the pantry. That and crackers, as well as baby carrots in the fridge. She liked to munch.

He sat down with a finger of good scotch, plus a cup of hot tea.

"Taking your own advice." She smiled at him.

"A relaxer. I think I'm more upset than you are. All I can think about is, you missed the killer by minutes. He was still alive, so I think you're right about the timeline."

"If it weren't for the dogs, I never would have found him." She described Tucker barking, pulling on her jeans.

Fair looked down. "Good dogs." Taking a sip, he asked, "Were there signs of a struggle?"

"I could see footprints, sliding in the dust back there. His hand was sliced. As I waited for the emergency crew, ten minutes, I looked around for anything that could have been dropped, a handkerchief, a penknife. The attack looked like it was done with a big knife. Didn't see anything like that."

"It's just as well. Let the sheriff's department investigate all that. You didn't get any blood on you, so it seems he didn't bleed much. That would have been . . . well, upsetting."

"When I found him, he was flat on his back. Funny, I didn't focus on the blood at first. I knelt down to see what I could do. He was breathing, then I noticed the blood on the front of his shirt, some on the jacket, as well as the deep cut across his right palm. I got blood on my hands as I pumped his heart. Wiped it off on the grass when the emergency crew arrived. Maybe I shouldn't have done that. I don't know. Fair, I wasn't thinking clearly. All I was thinking about was, could I save him. People can stop breathing and be brought back."

"You did all you could."

"What's going on? Yesterday bodies were found, old, but it was still a bit of a shake-up. And today, murder. Is this a coincidence?"

"I don't see how the long-apart deaths could be related. But it is terrible timing."

"But, honey, maybe it isn't. You were there when Sandy offered us money. An amount that any of us could use. Now he's dead. Maybe there's something about the schools that we don't know."

He touched her hand. "Apart from the development value, there isn't anything else there. Perhaps Sandy made a promise about that land and he realized he couldn't deliver. He might have lost an investor; we don't know who those people are. Do I think a sane person would kill over the development rights? No. But then again, there are crazies out there. Plus, we don't know the potential profit."

"What if he was innocent? I mean, what if someone thought he had money, threw him in a car, brought him to the schools, killed him, and took his money?"

"That's a big risk for a couple of dollars in your pocket." Fair finished his tea. "Given what you've described, he was taken there. Perhaps he was showing the possible development to someone. A partner? A potential investor? Remember, we don't know who is behind this. We know the one possible developer, Thanatos, but nothing more. And consider this, if that was the case, he knew this person and had no fear of him or her. Him, I think."

She processed this. "Yes. Yes, I think you're right about the lack of fear. You have to get close to stab someone." She shivered.

"Let's leave this to Rick and Cooper. They'll have insights we don't."

"I sure hope so." Her voice was faint.

"Honey, you did all you could. Don't be hard on yourself. Sandy was dying. Nobody could have saved him."

"I know." Her voice sounded weaker. "But to see him like that."

"Had to be awful. Whatever this is about, he either stood in the way of someone making a profit, or his failure to secure the land . . . which would have taken time, no matter what . . . enraged someone. Sandy never struck me as a person who was involved in criminal activity."

"If he was, I bet it'll come out."

"I hope so. Until we know more, this is unnerving." Fair felt Tucker nudge his hand. "You've had a Greenie."

"One more. It's good for my teeth, remember?"

Wordlessly, Fair got up, walked to the cabinet, pulled out two more Greenies plus two catnip-infused little fake mice.

"Sucker." Harry smiled at him.

"Look who's talking."

"Right."

Fair sat back down.

"Thanks for coming home. I feel better." Harry reached for his hand.

21

May 24, 2024

Friday

The sheriff's department had yellow tape preventing anyone from driving into the school spaces. The restoration group had an emergency meeting at Susan's house, away from downtown. Cooper, off work, as it was now early evening, was also present.

"Did anyone here have an argument with Sandy over his offer?" Cooper asked.

"No," they replied in unison.

Susan then asked, "Are you on duty?"

"No. But I'm your friend and neighbor. Anything I can glean from you might be helpful. You nor I have any idea what transpired behind the gym. The timing and the place of the murder created new problems."

"Boy, that's the truth," Tazio responded. "We're getting attention. Not the right kind."

"But he did come and make an offer?" Cooper asked.

"Yes. Jim knows. We went to him." Lucas wanted to be helpful, but felt useless.

"You don't think someone will accuse Harry of murder, do you?" Ned's lawyerly mind was working.

"Well, it's possible. She was the last person to be seen with him. But it's unlikely." Cooper took a deep breath. "One of the reasons it's unlikely is focusing on this might uncover things the murderer doesn't want people to know. It looks like this might have something to do with the land."

"What else could it be?" Fair looked Cooper right in the eyes, then scanned the group. "A development brings in money, creates other problems. What else is there?"

"If we knew, maybe we'd be closer to this murderer." Tazio then added, "I've been thinking. What if there's more than a development? I have no idea what that might be. What else could bring in money?"

"That's why the dead should be left alone." Harry then changed the subject slightly. "With Sandy's terrible end, we should ignore the possibility of more burial, even a potter's field, until some other time."

"You're right. We don't want the schools to seem like a hard place." Ned blew air out his nostrils.

"Right before our big day. No good can come of it." Harry stuck to her feelings about this.

"There is running water under that land." Fair had paid attention to the GPR findings. "Sandy had to know that."

"You mean literally digging could pollute the water? Wells downstream?" Lucas asked. "Any kind of development could create pollutants."

"There are developments between here and Chiles Orchard. They draw water up from individual wells." Tazio hadn't really thought about the water. "So far, no problems. That doesn't mean there isn't something we don't know."

Susan sat straighter. "Enough problems to be killed for them?"

"Sandy's murder is big news. It will stay big news, but we don't have to focus on it." Tazio only wanted to keep things stable, get the celebration off. Then they could focus on what might enhance or ruin a development.

"Jim may have ideas about Sandy's silent investor or investors," Ned added. "He is the mayor. He and I can recheck title transfers on the land."

"I keep coming back to what if there is more? We're focused on real estate development. Maybe this is something we never considered or even know about." Tazio had an odd feeling, provoked by Sandy's murder.

The room fell silent.

Lucas finally said, "It's not going to be easy to keep people away. Evil has a peculiar fascination. Murder is evil."

"Good point," Cooper agreed. "The fewer the people back there, the better."

"How long do you think it will be roped off?" Fair thought if someone on foot wanted to go past the yellow tape, it would be only too easy.

"I'd give it another day. We searched. Even used metal detectors. We looked for anything that could have been dropped. The doors to the gym were closed. Whoever did this knew to take Sandy behind the gym. If Sandy began to figure it out, he was too late," Cooper informed them.

"Yeah, but wouldn't you think Sandy would have screamed to save himself?" Susan wondered.

"I don't know. If he thought he was going to live, he obeyed. He was stabbed in the chest. The team called in as soon as they studied him. He knew who killed him. They were very close, and whoever it was, they were right-handed. Also, the killer knows the schools or made use of Sandy's knowledge."

"Murder brings people out of the woods, doesn't it?" Harry grimaced.

"Anything violent, a car wreck, a flood, fill in the blanks. People want to see it." Cooper knew of what she spoke.

"What else could be back there?" Lucas couldn't think of a thing. "I mean, if there was anything else of value, wouldn't someone know it by now? I'm trying to think of anything. You know, like gold or buried treasure. Far-fetched for twenty acres in Crozet. But it's possible other people have known."

Cooper again reminded them. "We gave it a pretty good going over. But both of the GPR operators did say there were areas . . . the one fellow said 'seams' . . . where the radar couldn't penetrate. He told us that was consistent with clay. Other properties also bounce back radar. Clay is obvious, because we have so much of it."

"Would anything valuable reveal itself? Just thinking. Like gold?"

"I'll ask, but neither of them mentioned that. As for some kind of treasure, it would probably be buried in a box. The radar picked up odd metal buttons. No boxes. We're stuck." Harry felt crestfallen.

"Did any of you have bad feelings about Sandy?" Cooper pressed a bit.

"No. He'd been interested in the place once the schoolhouses began to be properly restored. The place started to look better as we kept it up. We weedwacked and bush-hogged from the beginning." Harry was proud of their work. "Sandy was looking for a big profit. Maybe he wanted to live up to his father's real estate success and he involved the wrong people."

"Did anyone get the feeling he was under pressure? Maybe frightened?" Cooper hoped for any kind of clue.

"He was a little more aggressive than usual. I don't mean he was wooing us about the property but he was on it. You know? He dropped by a lot. But I never felt he was under pressure," Harry answered.

"He had no outstanding debts. No social drinking. No gambling. A clean slate. Very few complaints, although one couple did gripe that he kept showing them country estates they couldn't afford." Cooper slightly smiled. "Then again, how can a realtor get a sense of the client if they don't receive feedback?"

"I remember Sandy's father saying, 'Buyers are liars.'" Ned smiled.

"I suppose in a way, it's true. A couple tells you they want a Georgian house but falls in love with something modern. Then again, if you're a buyer, you don't know what you really want until you see it. I couldn't see it, but obviously Sandy saw something."

"Well, now everyone does. Maybe not homes around a park-like pasture, but the location is terrific. It's quiet. I expect the baseball diamond and football field might get some use." Tazio checked her watch. "You all, I have to drop off blueprints."

As she left amid a flurry of goodbyes, Cooper returned to her line of thinking. "Do you think Sandy's offer was genuine?"

A pause followed, until Susan broke it. "I wasn't certain about the amount, but yes, I did think he made a true offer."

"Has anyone else approached you all?" Cooper pressed.

"No. Not really. I mean, I've heard comments from people I know at the other real estate firms, complimenting us on our work, saying it would raise property values in town, but no offers." Susan then added, "Though any realtor will tell you, if you're ever ready to sell, let them know. Good business."

"Until it gets you killed," Harry said. "Maybe Sandy approached his investors long ago and said he could bring us around. Or maybe they approached him. There might be more people involved. Has anyone called and asked?"

"So it's possible his partners don't know?" Lucas found that unsettling.

"Could be." Cooper shrugged. "If anyone does contact you, of course come to me or Rick. All we know is, a longtime resident, well liked, was murdered. No apparent motive and no sign of the perp."

"Do you think we're safe?" Susan shivered.

"Yes. But again, we don't know why he was killed. That's why if anyone approaches you concerning the property, tell me. Immediately," Cooper emphasized.

22

May 25, 2024

Saturday

Mud House, a small eatery right by the railroad overpass, sat in a good location for Crozet. The parking proved adequate. Harry, Moz, Sherry, and Norton Sessions sat together. The TV station had interviewed Harry earlier concerning Sandy's death. She gave concise details. She also hated it. She couldn't avoid questions without casting a bad light on herself for not talking.

Why would she refuse to talk? From something like that people drew negative conclusions. Given the prevalence of the media in everyone's life, it was inconceivable for some people that another human being would not want to be the center of attention. Harry loathed it, but she looked relaxed as she told the reporter what had transpired.

Next up was Sheriff Shaw. As an old hand at this sort of thing, he declared she couldn't jeopardize the investigation and he was confident they would find the killer.

Moz, Sherry, and Norton had seen the news. They called Harry to meet at the Mud House, hoping to take her mind off her sorrowful event—if not sorrowful, then highly disturbing.

"So many of us know the buildings and the land. There are a lot of us that could have taken Sandy back there," Norton, a graduate of the Colored School, in his early eighties, said.

"I don't know. I hope not." Harry didn't want to talk about those bodies. "Norton, it's not like Sandy wasn't familiar with the place."

"On another subject," Sherry was sensitive to Harry's feelings, "everyone have their speeches?"

"Well . . ." Moz didn't answer.

"He wants it to be perfect," Sherry replied for him. "What about you?"

Norton, a happy expression on his lined face, said, "Think I've got it. What took me a long time is the fact that there were so many different tribes at our school. We had traces of everything but the tribes from the West. We just didn't discuss our heritage in school."

"Nobody did," Moz joined in. "What I thought about when I was a kid was making the football team and then, in the spring, track and field. Then when I became a coach, I zeroed in on athletic ability as well as the ability to listen to your coach. We didn't focus on race, because that was life. You know what I mean?"

Norton nodded. "We didn't talk about it much at home, except my father wanted my sisters and me to know who we were. So we did go to powwows, listened to stories from our people, stories of the fighting between the Algonquin-speaking peoples and those of us who were Sioux speakers. We are Cherokees. Lots of intermarriages. Tribal affiliation wasn't in the forefront of my mind, which disappointed my father. Also we never used the term *Native Americans.* We identified by our tribe."

Harry smiled. "I expect each of our parents were surprised at our interest or lack of interests. I suppose that's what being a parent entails. That and accepting that your kid is going to change dreams a lot. One week it's a football player. The next week a singer. Everyone tries out ideas about work, who they want to be."

Sherry laughed. "I wanted to sing like Ella Fitzgerald. I finally realized there is only one Ella, but I did love history and that I could do. What did you want to be, Norton?"

"A senator. Politics fascinated me. Once I graduated from high school, I did realize that a Cherokee person was not going to be elected a senator from Virginia. So I, like Sherry, turned to what I liked and had some ability for, which was car repair. Loved engines and still do."

"Your business has done very well," Harry complimented him.

"I worked for good people and then I went out on my own. Pop helped me. Gave me some of his savings to buy my first garage. My goal was for every car or truck that left my shop to run better."

"You succeeded." Moz smiled. "You were honest, Norton. How's your grandson doing?"

"Good. Mechanical ability runs in the family. I'll bet you I've had my head under the hood of just about every car made, from a Skoda to a Ferrari. Granted, I didn't work on the Ferrari, but I told the owner what I thought the problem was so he could be wary when he drove to Washington, D.C., to the dealer. Incredible car."

Harry, who also liked cars, trucks, tractors, asked him, "What's your favorite car?"

"Of all time?" Norton asked, and she nodded. "For looks, the 1961 Corvette. For a solid engine, any Dodge product with the old straight six. A helluva reliable engine. Held up, too. Now, well, the engines are fabulous, but too many computer chips for me. I want to drive the car, not have a computer do it."

"Me too," Moz enthusiastically agreed. "My Firebird is still a dream. I want a manual shift. And I want the high beam to be a button in the left side of the driver's floor. I hate all this stuff on the stalk of the steering wheel."

"Honey, I know you are right," Sherry touched his forearm, "but I love my Camry. I can get in and out of tight spots. I like the interior, and what goes wrong?"

"There is that," Harry agreed with her.

"Harry, what do you think will happen at the celebration?" Moz asked her. "Because of the murder. Think people will stay away?"

"Not at all. I think they'll come, listen, eat, and drink, and everyone will have to go by the gym. The murder site will be a big draw. People can't help themselves."

"You were good on the air today," Sherry complimented her. "Do you mind talking about it?"

"Finding him?"

"Not so much that, but what you think is going on?" Sherry responded.

"The only thing I can think about is the offer on the land. Maybe Sandy screwed up somehow. I don't fully know what his involvement was, other than offering to buy it as well as buy those of us off who did the work."

The others had heard of this. Sandy proved not to be as discreet as he might have been. He chatted up all people who might have insight into the schools, but especially the committee.

Moz raised his eyebrows. "I hope some of this dies down. Before I forget, those of us still alive who graduated from the high school, or who attended just the grade school, have voted on a name to honor someone. But I'm not telling." He grinned, then added, "We can't eradicate Plecker, but we can celebrate someone who helped us."

Harry smiled. "That's a great idea."

"It is," Sherry agreed.

"Do you have any thoughts about the land?" Harry asked Norton.

"No. Well, my father and other people used to talk when I was young about how our people, as well as other tribes, mined. There were some copper mines, and you know the thought now about the Lost Colony is that they were stolen and lived. Men were made to work in an iron mine. The women married the young men. That's how they got blue-eyed Indians, as the English reported later. Everyone thinks we were Stone Age people, but we knew valuable metals. We didn't have the tools to build with them, but think about it, copper conducts heat. People had to know that."

"Wasn't the first gold rush in Dalonegha, Georgia, in 1828?" Moz asked his wife. "The tribes had to know."

"Yes. There are still gold seams there. I would assume most of it is played out, or there still would be a big mine there. If something is valuable, people dig."

"A development is quite valuable," Norton piped up again. "It wouldn't be as difficult as mining, not that I think there's anything to mine there. Don't you think we'd know by now? Has to be the development."

"But to kill someone over it?" Sherry shook her head.

"If he was? Maybe he was stealing or blackmailing someone," Moz added.

"He always seemed like a nice guy." Norton knew him well, as Sandy and his father used his services.

"But don't the best criminals seem like nice guys?" Sherry tapped her fork on the plate. "John Dillinger. Even someone like Epstein. To my way of thinking, he trafficked more women at a high level because he was likable. Handsome, obviously good company, threw great parties. Why would people look beneath the surface?"

"True," Harry agreed. "Norton, did you know people named Raiselle? I ask because it's been my bad luck to find two bodies. Lucas and I had a car hauled up out of Swift Creek, and it contained Denver Raiselle."

"Oh yes." Norton nodded. "Made the news for two minutes. If that was a crime, it was long ago."

Nodding, Harry added, "But creepy nonetheless."

"Why would I know them?" Norton asked.

"I'm sorry. Denver Raiselle was part of the Monacan group at Bear Mountain in Amherst County."

Norton shook his head. "No. No one by that name when I was young, but one of the good things about today is that people will claim their heritage. No family by that name that I can think of though. Then again, until recently many of my people would pass as white."

"I try not to judge." Sherry put her fork down. "Who knows what you'll do if you have an advantage others don't? And Norton is right, it does make life easier if you can pass, even today."

"You know, I don't think of myself as a prejudiced person, but there's so much I don't think about because I don't have to think about it," Harry confessed.

"Honey, we're all that way," Sherry soothingly said. "Human nature. What do we first see? Someone's outside. No one knows what's going on inside. And thanks to our age, we were all drilled in how to look. What was feminine? What was masculine. You'd better fit it. When I think about it now, I realize how exhausting it was. I mean, I hated my hair. Then I couldn't stand my nose. I thought it was too big. Then I learned to really love my hair. And I don't know one woman who doesn't think she should lose at least five pounds."

Harry laughed. "Well, some of us certainly could."

"Are you picking on Susan again?" Sherry needled her.

"No. When she went on that diet, years ago, the exercise routine, she really lost weight. Every now and then she'll gain back a few pounds. Panics. Goes on another diet."

"See." Sherry held up her hands.

"What about you guys?" Harry asked them.

"You first, Moz," Norton teased him.

"When I was a little kid I wanted muscles. Looked at pictures of Joe Louis. Then I started growing, playing any sport I could, and got the muscles."

"Still have them, my angel." Sherry grinned at him.

"She's right, Moz. You have gray hair, but otherwise you still look like a jock," Harry agreed with Sherry.

"Never stopped. I work out, walk. It's up to you." Moz was proof of his beliefs. "Your turn, Norton."

"Oh . . ." A long pause followed this. "Skinny. I was always skinny until married, and lo and behold, a pot gut appeared. I don't have discipline, Moz. Now I've put on a little weight, so my pot gut doesn't look so strange. I was never athletic. My wife takes care of her appearance. She's five years younger than I am. I tell her she looks great, but she still frets over her looks. It's a waste of time; course, that's what you girls are saying."

"Norton, we don't care." Harry laughed at him. "I'm in my mid-forties now, and actually I'm beginning to like being a girl."

"Wait until you reach my age, honey." Sherry's laugh was infectious.

"Well, have to go put the horses up. It hasn't been warm enough to switch to scheduling them out in the day, in at night. Slow spring. But since we've been talking about looks, may I ask you all a favor?"

"Of course," they chimed.

"Lucas, of whom I have become quite fond, works at Aunt Tally's place. I think you know that, and he does outside stuff for her, sits and listens to her stories. He has such a good heart. He doesn't know many people. He needs a girlfriend. If you all know someone, maybe in her forties, open-minded and bright—Lucas is pretty smart—perhaps we all could figure out a way for them to meet. Something where it isn't obvious."

"Like at the celebration?" Sherry was already on it.

"Perfect." Harry's eyes lit up. "He'll be escorting Aunt Tally."

"How do you think he'd feel about a divorcee?" Sherry was making mental notes.

"Don't think he'd care," Harry answered.

"I'm sure we can come up with something."

As they left Mud House, Harry and Sherry walked together.

"Are you okay, Harry?" the older, kind woman inquired.

"Sort of. A little shaken, but Sherry, I can't for the life of me understand this. What is going on?"

"Sooner or later it will come out. It always does. Just take care of yourself."

"Thanks, Sherry. Thanks for thinking of me."

"You've had a shock. I haven't had anything happen and I'm even a bit nervous. Something like that right here in Crozet." Sherry sighed. "Maybe thinking you're safe is an illusion. Anything can happen at any time."

23

May 26, 2024

Sunday

The Very Reverend Herbert Jones tied his sermons to the ecclesiastical calender, as did most priests and pastors. Even into the early twentieth century, the church calender determined activities, discussions. By the early twenty-first century that structure slipped away for millions of people.

Harry, Fair, Susan, and Ned, all Lutherans, shared the same pew. The day was Pentecost, or Whitsunday, the day that the wind, fire, and a dove visited the disciples. It was the fiftieth day after Easter.

Reverend Jones did not focus on the physical elements of the day but on what questions might have crossed the minds of the disciples, who by this time had been through emotional extremes. He had a way of reaching into people's everyday lives that made his sermons compelling. He spoke to them not as a superior or even as a man of God, but as their friend, as another foot soldier in the chaos of life.

The sermon asked the parishioner, "How do you find your way?

Perhaps you, too, will speak in tongues or feel a great wind as the Holy Spirit enters the room. Then again, that was an extraordinary time and we would like to follow the Lord, but we are not the twelve disciples."

People perked up. *Yes, well, how do you know you're on the right path?*

Reverend Jones wove the gospel for the day, John 14: 23–31, into daily life.

Harry listened intently. When the gospel reading identified the Holy Ghost as a comforter, she never really understood the Holy Ghost. But then she heard, "Peace I leave with you, my peace I give unto you: not as the world giveth, give I unto you. Let not your heart be troubled, neither let it be afraid."

Fair felt her hand slide into his as she reached for him. She squeezed his hand.

After the service on this breezy, beautiful day, they walked out onto the exquisite grounds of St. Luke's. The harmony of the place invited walks. Often people would stop under the arcades after leaving the church building, to chat, to catch up, and many times to compare notes on the sermon.

The Very Reverend Herbert Jones had been serving his flock for decades. He was now in his eighties, and everyone realized how much he had given them, and also that the end to that time might be drawing nigh.

Cooper, not a churchgoer, started once she bought Herb's homeplace. Something about tending the sleeping family, generations of them, pushed her toward St. Luke's.

The group stopped down by the St. Luke's graveyard, early parish owners from the 1780s sleeping there. The living sat on the stone wall, the grass now lush green in front of them.

"Do you all understand the Holy Ghost?" Harry looked out at the lovely tombstones, the past right in front of her. There were people in there she knew. Her mother and father, her grandparents, their friends, and there were also people in there like Charles West, the architect, a former captured British soldier from the Revolutionary

War. Given the way he fashioned the buildings, the lawn, and the graveyard, she felt she would love to have met him. Surviving a war changed one. Somehow he found beauty.

"No," Fair answered. "I was confused. But hearing Reverend Jones read the gospel where the Spirit is designated a comforter, that begins to make sense. But I still want to see Him."

"Me too," Ned chimed in. "I'm a Lutheran. I believe in Martin Luther's cleansing of the church. I'm sorry it split Christendom, but I believe he was right. That doesn't mean I comprehend everything, and a God in Three Persons is beyond my powers."

Susan nodded. "But don't we understand our heart not being troubled, not being afraid?"

They all agreed.

"You know what I fear?" Harry came out with it. "Human evil. When I'm with the cats, dogs, and horses, I never feel evil. But when I read or see what people have done, I see it, I feel it, and I also feel helpless."

Cooper, usually quiet in such a discussion, said, "I see so much of it." Then she gestured toward the deceased. "Some of these people saw a great deal, others not so much. There are combatants from the Revolutionary War, the War of 1812, the War of 1861 to 1865, the Spanish-American War, World War I, World War II, Korea, Vietnam, the Mideast. So many wars."

"And those are only the declared ones. Right?" Harry asked. "Maybe we're born a blank sheet and the world writes on us."

"Harry, that's a passive view. You're the last person to be passive," Susan chided her.

"Oh, maybe I just feel helpless."

The three cats, sitting in Reverend Jones's office, watched people walking over the back lawns and could see the group sitting on the stone enclosure.

"Must have been a good sermon," Lucy Fur declared.

Cazenovia responded, *"Because so many are walking around? Talking?"*

Elocution opened one eye. "*Our help makes the difference. It's important to sit on his papers.*"

"*True,*" Lucy Fur agreed.

"*Aren't you glad we don't need sermons?*" Elocution licked her paw.

"*We never left the Garden of Eden,*" Cazenovia said with conviction. "*How many times have we heard Poppy or others talk about that garden?*"

The three soon left that off to discuss the cardinal family banging in the ivy growing on the arcade walls.

"*So noisy.*" Lucy Fur shook her head. "*They have all those trees out there in which to nest but they want to do it right here to disturb me. The only bird more big-mouthed than a cardinal is a bluejay.*"

"*He puts the food by these windows,*" Cazenovia rightly noticed. "*So why trouble yourself to go far? This way all they have to do is drop down.*"

"*Ha.*" the other two laughed.

As the cats solved many problems, the humans tried to solve theirs. Big Mim and Jim Sanburne, hand in hand, walked down to the graveyard. Seeing the Haristeens, Tuckers, and Cooper, they stopped by.

"This is such a peaceful place." Big Mim smiled. "I'll never tire of it."

All agreed. The Sanburnes also sat down. The group discussed Aunt Tally, how good she looked. How good Lucas was for her. They also reviewed the sermon. Reverend Jones had touched a chord. And then more mundane issues, like the falling price of lumber, interested them.

"It's falling," Harry agreed. "Good for most of us, but it means construction has slowed."

Jim folded his hands across his chest. "It's dominos, I think. You touch one and another falls or wobbles. Economists create grand theories about all this. It comes down to your bills. Everyone's bills. Do I care if this is Keynesian economics or Milton Friedman? No. I care about my electric bill."

They all jumped in. Everyone agreed, but Ned, who usually stepped back, reminded them, "Theory, true or twisted, gives us another way of looking at things. So while much of it seems foolish, out of touch, I think we still need it."

"Like dogma?" Harry asked.

A pause followed this. "It gets us in trouble." Fair sighed.

"It does," Ned agreed. "But if we choose not to get emotional, it helps us sift through the debris of life."

"Well, I'm sifting through a lot." Harry smiled.

Big Mim looked at Harry. "'Let not thy heart be troubled.' Harry, I expect your heart is troubled."

Harry's lips twitched for a moment then she answered honestly, "It is. I don't want to refute today's gospel, but I'm confused, troubled, and maybe a touch afraid. We all knew Sandy. Can anyone think of something he could have done? Or didn't do?"

"He made a lot of money with Hickory Real Estate. He would have made another fortune with a development, but other than that, I can't imagine anything." Fair liked Sandy.

"It makes me wonder." Susan carefully chose her words. "We've lived together for decades. Some of us have known one another all our lives. But do we *truly* know one another?"

Big Mim replied, "Do we know ourselves?"

"There's a topic." Ned smiled, and they were off and running.

Driving home, Fair at the wheel, Harry glanced at her husband's handsome profile. "One of the things I love about our friends is everyone thinks. Makes me think."

24

May 27, 2024

Monday

Aunt Tally loved holidays. Memorial Day meant the start of social summer, as opposed to June 21, the summer solstice. Big Mim arranged a party at her house, including her aunt, Lucas, and Teresa. Given Jim's position as mayor, many people were invited. It was casual, so they could stop by at any time. Each year people looked forward to this day.

Memorial Day started in the morning with a salute to the flag, a gun salute, then the high school band marching down Main Street, ending at the post office. The band was preceded by men and women dressed in Revolutionary uniforms, playing the drums and fifes. Everyone marched in smart order. When that was completed, people headed toward their Memorial Day parties. More steak was probably consumed that day than any other day of the year—at least it felt that way.

Harry and Fair turned down the long tree-lined drive to Mim's impressive estate, in the family for centuries, starting in 1792. The trees towered up to at least three stories, creating shade as well as giving one a secure feeling.

Overhead, a startling blue sky promised another reason to party.

"Beautiful as this place is, every time we come here, I look at the fencing and calculate the cost." Harry noticed a growing foal in the paddock closest to the impressive barn that, too, was built just before 1800. "That's a little beauty."

"Big Mim knows her stuff, but any form of breeding remains as much luck as brains."

"Just look at people." She laughed. "Everyone in town must be here. We'll park in East Jesus." She used the Virginia expression that meant far away. "The walk will do me good. Wore my flats."

"Honey, you always wear flats."

"Every now and then I totter around in my heels."

He parked, walked around and opened her door, which he always did unless they were in a big hurry. "Madam."

"Ah, thank you." She stepped out onto the grass, as they'd parked in a pasture. "I'm going to keep my light jacket on. It's a little coolish. If it's warm in the sun, I'll hang it on a tree limb. That will give Big Mim something to look at."

"I doubt she needs a focus. She has a good crop of foals this year. You know, it is a tiny bit cool. What an unusual May."

"Last time I wore this jacket was when I was walking the acres behind the schools and found the belt buckle. It's loose and I like the color. Basically, it's a thin red barn jacket."

"Looks good on you. But then, everything does."

"Honey, you're full of compliments."

They walked up toward the house, people coming forward to greet them even before they reached the food and drink or greeted the host and hostess.

Tazio and Paul waved them closer. "Big Mim has the best parties," Tazio enthused.

"Paul, the foals look good," Harry praised him.

Running a Thoroughbred barn, or any barn, is a lot of responsibility.

Paul smiled. "Thank you. Mim has such great mares. Sure makes my job easier. And she steers clear of the hot bloodlines. It's safer for me."

"That she does," Fair agreed.

They warmed to their subject, as does any horseman, while Carolyn Maki, another horseman, came over. Then came Lynne Beegle Gephard; her husband, Mark; Polly Bance, a master from Deep Run Hunt; and Caroline Eichler, another Deep Run master. Soon a flock of horse people were comparing notes, laughing, predicting a summer drought, wondering how hot it would get.

Finally, Polly looked at the Haristeens. "Come on, let's get you all food. You know no one will ever shut up."

Everyone laughed and the horse group broke up, but would eventually get back together. Whether horses were a passion or an obsession was up for debate, but the gang sure had a good time.

Polly was sidetracked by people she hadn't seen in months from Warrenton. Mim's party was a big draw.

Fair got a Perrier with lime for his wife and grabbed a cold beer for himself. He tipped the bartender, as he should.

The bartenders for these events were local men, usually, and some women, both of whom found the cash helpful. There were four bartenders at the two bars at either end of the patio behind the house. It was more English than a patio, but Jim and Paul put out chairs. One can tire standing.

In the middle of the group was Aunt Tally, with Teresa by her wheelchair on one side and Lucas on the other. Moz and Sherry were talking to her with a lot of animation.

"Are you hungry, sweetie?" Fair asked.

"Not just yet, but it is Memorial Day, and I will need a hot dog soon. Can't have the day without a hot dog. Can't have Fourth of

July without a hot dog either." Harry liked holidays as much as Aunt Tally did.

Miranda Hogendobber was there, so Harry hurried to her. "How are you?"

The two former co-workers caught up, then Miranda was pulled away by one of her choir members from the Church of Holy Light.

Fair said, "I'm going over to Moz and Sherry for a minute. I see Jennifer Nesbitt flagging you down. You two will compare hunter-pace notes," he added, mentioning an outdoor course with lots of jumps and an undisclosed optimum time.

Foxhunters loved hunter paces after hunt season was over, and Jennifer rode a spectacular mare that she had bred.

Harry looked around, realizing that her life was in front of her. She had known most of these people for decades, and of course she and Susan were in the cradle together. Their mothers would put them in, hoping they'd sleep. As they grew, their mothers dumped them in the sandbox in the summers. Of course, they covered each other in sand.

"Harry." Aunt Tally waved her hand.

Moz and Sherry turned around. "Harry."

Happy to see her friends, she went over. "Isn't this a perfect day?"

"It is." Aunt Tally took the drink Teresa handed her. Had a tiny shot of smooth, smooth bourbon, which Aunt Tally cherished.

One had to alter one's drinking habits with age, and she did, but there were times when a girl needed a party even if she was 103.

"You missed a good sermon yesterday. Which reminds me, is Reverend Jones here?" Harry asked.

Moz pointed to the farther bar, where the good reverend was standing with a bunch of men, most of whom had served in our armed forces. The reverend had been a captain in Vietnam. So many men who had seen combat gravitated to him.

"Doesn't he look great?" Sherry noted. "I mean, he's in his eighties now, so he's youngish, you know."

They all laughed.

Lucas waved his hand. "No one here looks their age. Healthy people."

Sherry grinned. "We are."

Aunt Tally tapped her wheelchair wheel. "Remember, I can run anyone down. I may be the oldest, but I can still get you."

They were laughing and joking. Teresa, too, though as Aunt Tally's nurse, she was often quiet, circumspect; but this was a great day.

"Oh, Ashley." Sherry waved.

Seeing Ashley walk over to her great-aunt, it was obvious they were related. Same oval face, high cheekbones, full lips, sparkling brown eyes, creamy skin. Ashley had a few smile lines, but she was like Sherry, a good-looking woman with a feminine body.

"Aunt Sherry," Ashley said.

"Sugar, you remember Harry. This is Teresa Becker, and the blond fellow is Lucas Harkness."

Ashley stretched out her hand, which Lucas took. They talked to everyone, and then the two of them got caught up in their own conversation.

Sherry raised her eyebrows. It was obvious they hit it off. Harry, looking at her, winked. She liked seeing Lucas, a bit shy, be engaged with a new person. Sherry had kept her promise to see if she could find someone for Lucas.

Aunt Tally looked around. People lined up to greet her, so the group around her stepped back.

Teresa, seeing Lucas opening up, kindly told him, "Take a break. I'll watch her."

"Have you ever seen the stables?" Lucas asked Ashley.

"No, I haven't."

"If you'd like, I'll show you. Aunt Tally's family built this place in 1792." He walked beside her. "Over time they added to it, but the house and the main stables were built at the same time."

Harry and Sherry watched the two walk off.

"She'll get a history lesson." Harry laughed.

"Ashley's like me, a History teacher in Richmond."

"Sherry, educating others runs in your family." Harry very much admired Sherry.

"It does. My mother used to always quote, 'The past is present.' I believe it is."

"I do, too. Doesn't mean I understand it. Oh, here comes our favorite pastor."

"Girls." Reverend Jones opened his arms to embrace them both. "I mean, ladies. You both look wonderful."

"That was a terrific sermon yesterday morning." Harry added, "Made me think."

"Made me think, too." He grinned. "Sherry, what are you reading? Whatever it is I know I should be reading it, too."

"*The Tyranny of Merit.*" She then briefly explained the book.

As the two talked, Armand Neff walked up. "The best party. The best people." He held up his glass.

"Armand, you are so smooth," Aunt Tally teased him.

"Moz, your team is okay, but not knocking the ball out of the park."

"Armand, it's the beginning of the season. The Cards will do great."

As the men argued baseball, more people came up to Aunt Tally. Sherry and Harry stepped farther back.

Armand came up to Harry. "Are you okay?" he asked, then added, "Are you two ready for the celebration?"

"We'd better be. You'll be there, of course." The two women looked at each other as Harry spoke. "And yes, I'm more or less okay. I try not to dwell on Sandy's murder."

"I can't believe the celebration's almost upon us." Sherry slid away from the Sandy topic. She wished Armand hadn't brought it up by asking Harry if she was okay.

Harry reached in her pocket absentmindedly, pulled out the bluestone she'd picked up when she found the buckle. "Forgot all about this."

"Where'd you find that?" Armand inquired.

"On the back acres. It's pretty, isn't it? Those blue flecks sparkle." She dropped it in his hand.

"You never know what you'll find." He inspected it. "Who knows what is under us, what the glacier pushed, what's in the mountains themselves? We know some of it, but there are always discoveries as technology advances."

"Don't you think that's why the Monacans, the Appamatuck, and the other tribes that lived by the mountains, here or in the valley, did so well? I guess you could say in their day they were rich," Harry posited.

"Think you're right." Armand noticed Lucas and Ashley leaning over a fence at the main barn. "Who is that terrific-looking woman?"

"My great-niece," Sherry answered.

"I should have known." He cocked his head toward her, then took a deep breath. "It's odd to be at a big party and Sandy isn't here. I don't think that man had missed a party since kindergarten."

Harry, again not wishing to recall her time with Sandy's last moments, demurred. "Maybe where he is now they are having the best parties ever."

Sherry picked up on it. "Like the Cloth of Gold in 1520."

"I can't keep up with you." He finished his drink.

"You would have been in your element. Kings, Francis I and Henry VIII. Beautiful women, sporting contests, endless food and drink. Entertainment, sumptuous jewels. Tents that were so beautiful you could live in them."

"Could it be I was born in the wrong century?" He sighed in mock despair. "I'll just make the best of it."

As he walked off to greet business buddies and their wives, Sherry looked down at the barn and the paddock where Lucas and Ashley stood. "She's had a hard knock. If nothing else, they'll be friends, I think."

"What happened to Ashley?"

"Four years ago her husband was killed in an auto accident on the turnoff to Broad Street from 64. Boom. She began to take an interest in life after two years, but not a lot of interest in men. Barton, her husband, was very intelligent and such a gentle soul. All the men she would meet wanted to impress her with . . . what, how manly they are? Revolted her. Now, granted, she could have overreacted, but all those men tried to impress her."

"I see. I think the men who have to tell you how manly they are aren't. You know?"

"I do. I married a real man and so did you. My big brute of a husband is so sweet, so loving. If a bird falls out of the nest, he has to pick it up and climb up to put it back in."

"Fair's a big softie, too, and then I watch him pick up something that weighs two hundred pounds like it's fifty. But Sherry, maybe our husbands don't have to prove anything because they are physically powerful."

"I've thought of that." Sherry smiled. "And I'm very glad I'm a woman. I don't have to prove I'm a woman."

They both laughed, then Harry said, "Maybe we don't know how lucky we are."

25

May 28, 2024

Tuesday

The morning sparkled, a slight breeze lifted the scent from flowering apple trees across the field. Harry, Susan, Tazio, and Lucas arrived early. They sat in the high school building, which glowed with early light. Mrs. Murphy, Pewter, Tucker, and Pirate kept them company.

Susan rose, hearing a motor. "What's a car doing here?" She turned to the others, sitting at the school desks. "You all, there are cars coming down the drive."

Tazio stood up and joined her at the window. Parked by the gym were three cars, one of which was the county sheriff's squad car.

Harry and Lucas came to the window.

"Someone drove to work this morning, saw the sheriff's car, and must have told their friends," Harry said.

"Told them what?" Lucas figured it out as the words left his mouth. "Another murder?"

Harry put her hand on the window, removed it, pulled a work

handkerchief out of her pocket, and wiped the window. "Never underestimate the power of gossip."

"What should we do?" Susan asked.

"Nothing. This is the sheriff's call. I see Mud House lunch people, Bluebird Bookstore people, every realtor in town, and let us not forget the fire chief." Susan started laughing. Even Armand Neff was there.

"Maybe Rick called the fire chief." Harry considered him a valuable, competent person.

Lucas grinned. "Here comes Jim Sanburne. Maybe he slept late."

"Not Jim." Susan smiled back. "He's here to chat with Rick and the other officers. It didn't occur to him, as it didn't to us, that this would be a draw. Not that anyone really knows what is going on. In their minds it must be the idea of fresh murder. There goes Jim, walking down to the group closest to us. He's talking to them. Rick's coming up from the far group."

"Looks like a high-level conference." Tazio lifted her eyebrows in amusement.

"So who do you want to bet will speak to the onlookers? Jim or Rick?" Harry challenged them.

"Jim. Everyone likes the mayor," Lucas said.

"My bet is Rick. No one will question the sheriff." Harry took the bet. "I bet a dollar."

They argued about the sum. Susan bet on Rick. Tazio bet on Jim.

"*Hear it?*" Pewter cocked her ears.

"*Yeah.*" Pirate lowered his head toward the floor.

"*The grade school mice.*" Mrs. Murphy liked the scurrying sound.

"*Seems the digging is arousing everyone, human or mouse. The crows are sitting in the trees, watching.*" Tucker was enjoying herself.

Sure enough, Sheriff Rick Shaw walked across the fields, which took five minutes. He was in no hurry. The onlookers did not walk toward him. What a mixed bag they were. Miranda Hogendobber had driven over to check on her plantings and to water them. Seeing the activity, she couldn't help but walk forward to where the other people were. Armand Neff stood next to Ingram Kiley, a burly fellow who rented ditch witches, big tractors. No doubt one had driven by, noticed the squad car, called the others.

"We'll take your money." Susan and Harry opened their hands toward Tazio and Lucas.

Harry, Susan, Tazio, and Lucas each observed the curiosity and nervousness of their neighbors. Well, why shouldn't they be curious? There had been a murder behind the gym. Gossip leaked out about an unnamed development company wanting to buy the acres by the schools. As usual, when no one has a firm answer, the suppositions could be imaginative.

One rumor was that foreign powers were behind this. Another was that there were treasures Crozet didn't know about. Claudius Crozet's tunnels through the mountains were only the beginning.

Rick reached the group. Lucas, thanks to his work in the State House, had some ability to read lips.

"What's he saying?" Susan leaned on him.

"'Hello.'" Lucas laughed, then continued. "'Folks, there has not been another murder. I know you are . . .' Can't make out that word. Uh." He squinted. "'We are double-checking the back acres before the celebration. There's an outside possibility that perhaps something, say a key chain, dropped. We went over the back of the gym building with a fine-tooth comb. I want to be sure I haven't missed anything.'"

Lucas exhaled. "No, not so bad. People aren't frowning."

Harry leaned on him from the other side. "You're now between Susan and me. And we have your dollar."

"It's very pleasant."

Tazio enjoyed the lightheartedness. So much was at stake for them with the schools. The years, the physical labor, the research, the appeals for help and materials and, lastly, finding the graduates, making certain every child who had attended the schools would be named. It became a passion for each of them. Over time they felt responsible for those former students and teachers. They did not want them forgotten, nor how they had been shunted away from larger school systems. It became more than the white schools versus the "colored" schools. It pushed them toward thinking about justice, injustice, and mostly a deep admiration for the teachers who instilled in their charges not just reading, writing, and arithmetic, but pride in who they were, discipline, and dreams. There were times when Tazio would get home and fight back the tears. After all, had she been born during those times, she would have attended these schools.

Harry looked down at the dogs. The cats perched on the desks. "Lots going on."

"We know," Tucker replied.

"Well?" Susan drawled out.

"They're leaving." Tazio breathed out. "I didn't expect trouble, but I also didn't expect this. Then again, our cars were here even before the law enforcement people. I'm sure some of the crowd recognized our cars."

As it was, Rick arrived first. He came into the school building, chatted with them a bit, and when the first truck arrived with the men to again scour the land, he popped back out.

Miranda knocked on the school door, opened it a crack. "Yoohoo."

"Come on in," Tazio said.

"Armand is behind me." Miranda smiled.

"He can come in, too," Tazio repeated the invitation.

"I saw your cars—well, Harry, your truck—and I thought I'd check the plants and then find you and everyone." Miranda stepped to the side to let Armand in.

Tazio gestured toward the chairs. "Sit down."

"Oh, thank you, no. Best I get out of the way." The sweet old lady turned for the door.

"Miranda, you aren't in the way. Who was to know that people would show up?"

Armand sat at a school desk as Pewter headed for the back of the room. Mrs. Murphy hesitated then followed her. "Well, I saw the cars, the squad car, and thought, 'Oh no.'" Miranda grimaced. "Not a good thought."

"Bet other people thought that," Lucas agreed.

"It is on people's minds." Armand tried to cross one knee over the other, but the desk was too small.

"They were for kids," Harry teased him.

"Well. What the hell is going on? Sorry, Miranda, didn't mean to swear," Armand apologized.

"Quite all right. These days people say so much worse." She nodded.

"Pewter is on the prowl." Pirate hauled up his big body to investigate.

Armand looked around. "So much natural light. Have you tested the stove?"

"We have," Tazio answered. "It heats up the room fairly quickly. Remember, these buildings were put up before electricity. A potbellied stove could throw out the heat better than a fireplace. People built solid structures. We've worked here during the wild winter days and stayed warm. And the advantage of never losing electricity, and freezing, is wonderful. All this new construction is terrific, but it doesn't take into account what we do when the power fails."

"Buy a generator." Armand shrugged.

Lucas replied, "Needs to stay outside, and you need to fill it with gas. Besides, they are expensive."

Armand thought a moment. "As you know, my business takes me around the world. Much as I get tired of traveling, I learn not just about people, but how their companies create profit. I like representing them. And I see different ways to heat or cool. The Swedes have enormous porcelain stoves—I guess you'd call them stoves—that go to the ceiling. They are the same principle as a woodburning stove. When it's that cold, you can't afford to be without heat."

"Aha. I know he's behind that small bookcase," Pewter gloated.

"Leave the mouse there." Tucker was firm. *"You'll scare the people."*

"No." The gray cat spat.

The humans, unaware of the cat and mouse drama, nattered on.

"Well, really I'm off. Good to see you all." Miranda stood up. "I'm thinking about a few more peonies."

"Anything you do is gorgeous." Tazio smiled at her.

"Oh." Miranda blushed.

"Is it true, Miranda? Do you sing to plants?" Armand teased her.

"I do." She lifted her chin. "They all love 'Swing Low, Sweet Chariot.'"

As they laughed, Pewter got the mouse to run and the little creature sped out behind the door, across the floor, looking for another hiding place.

"*Surrender,*" Pewter ordered the mouse.

"*Never, fatty.*" The little fellow was fast.

"Oh my God." Armand blasted out from the desk, opened the door, and ran out.

Tazio quickly followed him. "Are you all right?"

Deeply embarrassed, he whispered, "I'm terrified of mice."

Tazio, not one to judge, nodded. "I think we have a few residents in the buildings."

"Well, I'll be going, but it was good to see you." Armand briskly walked away.

Miranda, not the least bit afraid, called to Pewter, "Come now, Pewter."

"*Hooray.*" The mouse reached the cold potbellied stove and scooted underneath.

"*You can't stay there forever.*" Pewter crouched in front of it.

Mrs. Murphy, also at the stove, tried a different approach. "*The humans think you're cute.*"

"*I don't care. I am not budging.*"

The two dogs joined the humans, who were laughing.

"I never thought of men being afraid of mice." Harry sat back down as Tazio came inside, closing the door.

"Oh, people have fears. Maybe inborn. You know," Lucas filled them in, "snakes, spiders, mice. I once dated a woman and we went to see an old Harry Hamlin movie. Those great early special effects, where Medusa slides across the floor and Perseus is hiding behind the pillar. You hear and see the rattles on her snaky tail, and you see all the snakes on her head. Anyone who looks at her is turned to stone. Well, my date, the poor thing, screamed and ran out of the theater."

"What did you do?" Susan tilted her head.

"Went out to find her. I don't know that I calmed her down, but I took her to dinner."

"Did she go out with you again?" Harry asked.

"No." Lucas laughed.

"All because of Medusa?" Tazio laughed, too.

They watched the cars drive out, sat down again, and talked. The Ground Penetrating Radar and metal detectors in the fields did not take long. The law enforcement men were well trained.

Sheriff Shaw knocked on the door. "Come in," Susan called out.

"No dropped knives, keys. We did find one soldier and, yes, he is wearing a Union buckle. Well, not wearing, but it was on his bones where a belt would be." Rick watched the two cats, immobile. "And the boys picked up what appears to be another adult male. The bodies were buried without caskets. This may have been a potter's field," Rick said, filling them in.

"Thanks for telling us. We're thinking about the celebration. There's no need to bring up that some indigent people are sleeping in the back." Tazio leaned on a desk. "Maybe later some recognition can be put up."

"Harry, are your cats frozen? They haven't moved," Rick asked.

"A mouse."

"Ah, well, best to take them out or we'll have another murder." The sheriff did have a sense of humor.

Later that evening, cats and dogs lazing in the living room, Fair and Harry sat close together on the old, comfortable sofa.

"Fair, what surprised me were the people there once they saw the squad cars. We stayed in the high school building. I didn't want any part of it. I can understand nosiness. Oh, Armand was there, and he and Miranda came into the classroom after Rick sent people off. She wasn't being nosy, she'd come to inspect her plants. And you won't believe this, the cats chased a mouse out from under the potbellied stove. Armand nearly screamed, then jumped from the desk and ran out of the building. A grown man."

"How do you know the mouse wasn't scared, too?"

They both laughed.

Pewter rolled over on her back, exposing an impressive underbelly. "*Terrified. The mouse was terrified of me.*"

26

May 29, 2024

Wednesday

"Rats." Harry stopped for a moment and reached up as the halter slipped off Shortro, one of her horses. He liked walking into his stall.

Cooper, leading Booper, an old mare, also stopped. "Need a hand?"

"No, I'll flip the lead rope around his neck. He's a sweetheart."

Shortro rubbed his head on Harry's arm. *"Here come those bad cats."*

Mrs. Murphy and Pewter sauntered out from the barn to watch the horses come in.

"Mother loves her horses." Pewter sniffed. *"All they do is eat and sleep. We work on the farm."*

"She rides them." Mrs. Murphy stated the obvious.

"So what? That can't be hard work. She doesn't weigh anything." Pewter thought her human should have more interest in food, more often.

As Harry and Cooper walked the two easy animals back to their stalls, the sun set behind the mountains.

"Getting more sunlight." Harry watched the long rays disappear, the land glowing with a golden dust. "Winter gets me. When the sun sets at four-thirty, I set with it. And I'm usually still working."

Cooper remarked, "Then the days get longer, but when we change to Daylight Saving Time, I'm still getting up in the darkness."

"Yeah, gets me, too."

Shortro bowed his head when Harry slipped off the lead rope. He would follow her even without it. He liked his stall.

Each one had about four flakes of good hay in the corner and one small scoop of grain. Every horse received a larger scoop in the mornings, and those who needed special vitamins got them dumped in their grain. Harry, particular about feed, vitamins, and special food for the horses, was also careful about their coats. The nights were warming. Not human warm, but horse warm. Usually in a hard winter every horse kept on their blanket. Today they wore no blankets. Their coats were shedding out. The mercury would dip to the mid-fifties, quite delightful for a horse, as well as dogs with heavy coats, also now shedding out. Humans needed a jacket, maybe a sweater.

"How do you get the shine on them?" Cooper asked.

"Grooming, but once they shed out, I'll slip a little corn oil in the food, like a tiny bottle-cap full, swirl it around. There are grooming things you can use. I try to keep stuff as natural as possible. They really don't need much. There is natural oil in their coats."

Finishing up in the aisle, the two women repaired to the tack room. The cats scooted through the wooden door, as did Tucker. Harry opened the door for Pirate. The animals circled a few times, dropped, happy to snooze.

"Need anything?" Harry asked.

"No." Cooper sat in a comfortable old chair, putting her feet up on an overturned bucket. "Oh, that feels good."

"Glad you dropped by. I needed an extra hand. Wore myself out with last-minute organizing for the schools, plus my garden. So much is late this year. Anyway, I'm sure you heard about yesterday."

Cooper lifted her right hand. "You know, we should have thought of that. Rick is intent on clearing some of this up. He has a good political sense. I think most sheriffs do. He's better than I am. But it never occurred to him, me, any of us that the squad car would draw a crowd. People are fascinated with outrageous acts though. If there was an app on your phone to show amputations, people would watch it. They'd watch people getting electrocuted. After all, once executions were public. I swear, if they were today, people would watch."

"Cooper, that's gross."

Her tall friend shrugged. "I didn't say it wasn't. Thought I would stop by to tell you we found nothing. Chances are slim we will find anything belonging to the killer. All we would find would be DNA. Even a piece of chewed gum might help."

Harry scooted forward in her chair. "Actually, I have no idea about any of this DNA stuff."

"I'm hardly an expert, but I have to take classes, upgrade my training. We have come so far. In a crisis, a body, bones, can be identified in about two hours now."

"Two hours!" Harry's eyebrows shot up.

"Think of a crisis where hundreds, maybe even more, of bodies are left. A tidal wave. An earthquake. Huge fires burning thousands of acres. Any major weather event qualifies as a catastrophe. As science has advanced, that's one area where identifying remains is critical. People are desperate to know if their families are alive, especially if they live in another area of the country. War, another catastrophe. Well, it can be done these days. For skeletons that are found, they use femurs. You do better with weight-bearing bone. A fragment is drilled, then cleaned. The people who do this are highly trained, obviously. They pulverize the fragment. The most common form of analysis is polymerase chain reaction. Works on degraded samples."

"That's a mouthful."

Cooper smiled. "It is, but the various tests look for DNA building blocks. They are searching for patterns in genetic material. Don't ask me what those are, but a PCR machine conducts tests simultaneously. We could find a relative of Denver Raiselle, speaking of old bones. Luckily, we found his wife."

"I wish something had turned up in the back, or another search where Sandy was murdered could reveal something." Harry sighed.

Cooper nodded. "What I'm waiting for is someone to show their colors. Someone to make another offer on the acres. Someone who perhaps was a silent investor. What has occurred to me, a long shot, is what if Denver Raiselle's murder is connected to something geological, even to Sandy's death? That's a long shot, but I went through my notes. I need a geologist in the technical stuff, so I focused on bills, invoices, everyday records. I found, as you know, bills sent to realtors for examining soil."

"I remember you mentioned that. Professor Raiselle had a good side business."

"I originally checked only the year in which he was killed, 2006. Then decided to look at a few prior years. Remember the time when many Europeans were moving to Virginia?"

"Kind of. I was wrapped up in working at the post office then, trying to keep the farm afloat, too. I'd been out of Smith for years. Of course, I was still grappling with the loss of Mom and Dad."

Harry's parents had been killed in a car accident when she was in college. Miranda Hogendobber got Harry the job when she graduated. Miranda's care and concern helped Harry greatly.

"That had to be awful," Cooper sympathized.

Harry nodded. "Great shocks knock you sideways. So many people were kind to me. Miranda, Aunt Tally, Big Mim, and Jim, and of course Fair. You get through. But I dimly remember the incoming tide of Europeans and some Africans."

"Anyone who doesn't think high taxes can drive people out isn't paying attention." Cooper remembered the economic crunch in Europe at the time. "As for South Africa, they also feared violence. Virginia is beautiful and stable. They snapped up a lot of property."

"So what did you find, Coop?"

"Professor Raiselle was flooded with work during those years. Some of his invoices were sent to Hickory Real Estate. Sandy's father, I assume."

"Funny, Sandy didn't want to take over his father's business. Once he realized there were no startup costs, though, I guess it made the decision easier. And he worked with his dad for five years before Martin, his father, retired," Harry recalled.

"There may be no connection at all." Cooper paused. "But who knows what Professor Raiselle found?"

"Once we're on the other side of the celebration, ask realtors from that era. Many are left."

"I will. When Sandy was murdered, of course, we questioned today's successful realtors. No one had any idea. But I'm going back to it."

"If I can help, you know I will," Harry offered.

"Thanks."

Harry looked at her neighbor and friend. "What troubles me is whoever committed this murder may not live in Crozet, but they were here, knew the area, and got away from the scene. My feeling, a terrible feeling, is that it's someone who lives . . . if not in Crozet then in Albemarle County."

"I think you're right." Cooper looked at the clock, fading light in the center aisle of the barn.

Harry glanced at the light, as well. "Do you ever feel a dip in your emotions when the sun sets, twilight?"

"Sometimes. We aren't meant to be out in darkness."

"Yes." Harry thought. "Maybe that's why it seems so bold to kill someone in broad daylight."

Cooper smiled. "You know, murder upsets people. Frightens them. Angers them. And yet it is the easiest crime to understand if it's done in a fit of anger. What's harder to understand is plotted murder. That truly is cold-blooded."

"That's the truth. Do you think if you're physically close to the victim, it's more emotional?"

"I can't spout statistics, but yes, I do. He had to be driven in the killer's car. His car was back at his house. Sandy's killing was somewhat thought out, too. The killer knew where to kill him. He was close, he used a knife, they knew each other."

"That narrows the list." Harry grimaced.

"It does. And yet we haven't one idea."

"Yet," Harry replied.

"Don't be the person that figures it out," Cooper directed her. "Just don't. Let it go, despite the shock of being there. Chances are you know the killer and he knows you. Don't tempt fate, Harry." She inhaled deeply. "We'll find him sooner or later. I'm wondering if this doesn't have something to do with the schools. Haven't found a connection, but it keeps crossing my mind." She paused. "The development is an obvious motive, but a company doesn't get to develop a property by killing the realtor."

"Maybe it isn't about the development."

"Ah." Cooper drew that out.

"I think of that line from *Hamlet*. 'There are more things in heaven and earth, Horatio, than are dreamt of in your philosophy.' "

Cooper stood up, stretching. "True. But again, don't play detective. Remember what happened to Hamlet."

27

May 30, 2024

Thursday

The ground, growing hard, as the area needed rain, felt like brick underfoot. Harry walked over the still green grass, marveling at how quickly the earth could bake then just as quickly dissolve into mud puddles. The Weather Channel predicted rain tomorrow. She hoped that would come to pass.

Her truck, parked behind the school buildings, wouldn't attract attention. She wanted to study the back acres without interruption. She wanted to imagine the development as explained by Sandy Rycroft. She also wanted to think about the baseball and football fields. Her mind was leaning toward community resources.

Mrs. Murphy, Pewter, Tucker, and Pirate tagged along, occasionally diverted by a tempting scent.

Harry knelt down. She attempted to dig her garden tool into the earth. But it was too hard, so she simply scraped the earth's surface, scratched a bit of dirt.

She saw a tiny bit of stone. Flicking the dirt away from it, she unearthed a pretty crystal about an inch in size. She pocketed it, then scratched around a bit more. She found a piece of shale near the surface, again small, the mica flecks glittering. She pocketed that, too.

Then she stood, reminding herself some old bones were underfoot. She pulled out the shale and crystal again. As there was a large shale operation in Buckingham County, there would be no point in creating one here if a shale seam lay underneath.

She remembered the GPR report about wave impulses not being absorbed. Clay could cause that, but so could shale. She'd been reading. For one thing, it fascinated her. For another, she considered that a precious metal could provoke murder. People would kill over gold and silver. But GPR did not identify anything of that nature. One would need to really dig in a pattern to establish what was down there.

She walked closer to the schools. Again she knelt down, hand-dug for samples. More quartz, gneiss, not a lot of rock. She got a bit deeper, coming up with clay. She knew the clay when she hit it. Felt like brick. No wonder there were so many brick houses in early Virginia. It was beautiful, soft red brick, too. Plus one could find it most anywhere, although rarely on the shoreline or around a big lake. She reminded herself, she wasn't a geologist. She didn't necessarily know what she was looking at or how it was formed.

"Bear." Tucker sniffed along the creek bed, eager to know what animals used the place.

"They're smart about moving around, finding food." Mrs. Murphy admired bears.

"Coyotes are here, too." Pirate knew the scent from Odin, a coyote behind Harry's farm who would sometimes visit.

Difficult as coyotes could be in a pack, Odin was mostly a loner. The dogs and he would talk sometimes in the early evening. The cats stayed out of it. If they were going to make friends with wildlife, it was with the opossum, Simon, who lived in the hayloft.

Harry dug more. Bits of stone, more crystals, but nothing that caught her attention. If she could admit it to herself, some of this digging was to take her mind off Sandy's murder. Or that the killer might be close.

Tucker, intent on the scent, moved along the creek banks.

With a grunt, Harry pushed off one knee to stand up. She walked, head down, to the creek bed.

Reaching the creek, running but not strong, she knelt again, leaning over a low spot to dig. The sand easily gave way. She kept at it, pulling up some very pretty quartz crystals. She nearly went headfirst as she plunged her little tool into the sand, water up to her forearm.

"Softer than I thought," she said to herself.

She pulled up sand, sat back, and pushed it around with her forefinger, pulling out a beautiful bluestone, much bluer than what she'd found weeks ago. She dipped them back in the water to clean them off.

Leaning over to wash the stone, she nearly fell into the creek face-first.

Pirate, noticing her struggle, trotted over, stepped into the creek to walk right in front of her. Grateful, she put her other hand on his neck, balanced herself, then stood up.

"Thanks, Pirate."

He jumped out, shaking himself all over her. She made a face but hugged him all the same.

Looking at the cleaned bluestone, she marveled at how beautiful it was.

That evening, after she and Fair finished a light supper, she put her finds in front of him.

"These crystals are pretty. Don't people think crystals have emotional properties?" he asked.

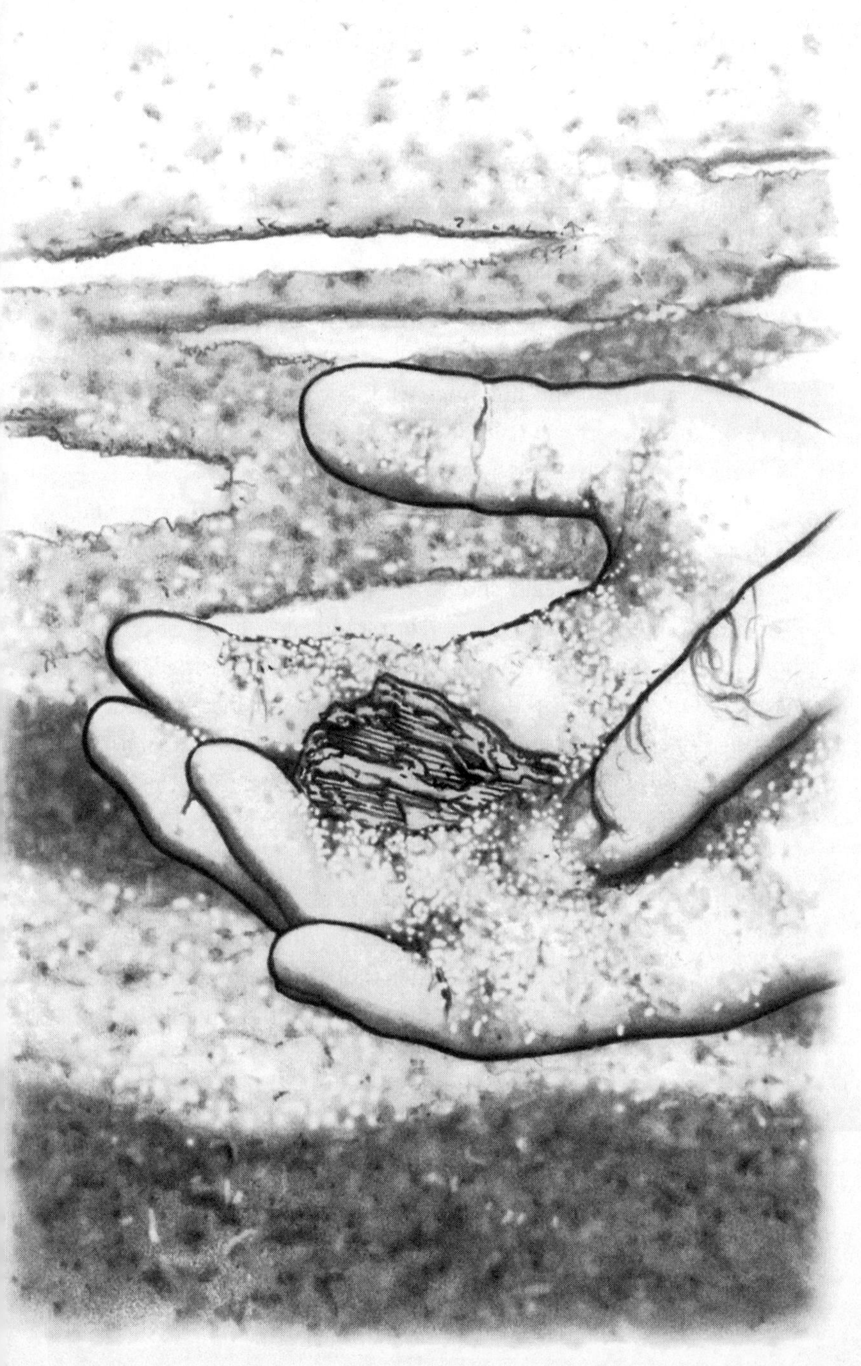

"So they say. Like scents can affect people's moods. Well, kind of the same."

"Do you believe it?"

She looked at her husband. "No, but if one believes it, I think it can help. People need to be calmed, feel safe. Right now I'm not sure any of us feel a hundred percent safe."

"You've got a point there." He pushed the sparkling finds around, as she had cleaned them again in the sink then dried them vigorously.

"I parked behind the buildings. Didn't want people to see me drive on the property. In truth, I didn't want to deal with anyone."

"Yes," he simply replied.

"None of this leads me anywhere. I wasn't expecting to find gold, but then again, I thought I might find something interesting, something of value. I really should accept the obvious."

"There is a lot of land value." He picked up a hunk of quartz, holding it to the light. "Amazing how this stuff is formed." Then he picked up a bit of the shale. "All of this is a product or result of the pressures of the mountains. I would think it's pressure, plus the movement of the glacier. If you think about it, much of the agricultural wealth of our country is the result of the glaciers pushing down all that rich Canadian soil."

"Even so, Alberta, Saskatchewan, they're pretty good for agriculture. Pretty flat, too, as is our Midwest. Here, different, we have two mountain chains themselves, the Shenandoah Valley and the undulating land on the east side of the Blue Ridge. Until it finally flattens out. Who knows what's under all this?"

"Makes me wish I'd taken a geology course in college." He examined the shale. "Those bits of mica sparkle, don't they?"

"Makes me want to see the marble quarries that Michelangelo used. How beautiful that stuff is. Another product of pressure, I assume. And how does one know what's remarkable, what you can bang at, and what isn't?"

"Fortunately Michelangelo did." Fair laughed.

Mrs. Murphy leapt onto Harry's lap, closed her eyes, and purred.

"When I was talking to Cooper yesterday, after we brought the horses in, I mentioned that famous line from *Hamlet*: 'There are more things in heaven and earth—' "

He finished it. " 'Horatio, than are dreamt of in your philosophy.' Great line."

"She told me not to get nosy and to remember what happened to Hamlet."

"She's right." He leaned back in the kitchen chair, stretching out his long legs.

"I kept turning things over in my mind and thought of the line from Emily Dickinson. 'Wonder is not precisely knowing/And not precisely knowing not.' I feel that way."

"You've been reading poetry again?" He smiled at her.

"No. Lines pop into my head, but I often think no poem is truly simple. They have to be so compressed, but that doesn't mean they're simple. Kind of like these crystals. Compressed. They shine." She shook her head, laughed at herself. "I promised to take a break till the celebration is over. Really."

"I'll hold you to it. Maybe we can slip away for a few days."

"You're not going anywhere without me," Tucker barked. *"They can't think clearly."*

"All you think about are bones." Pewter curled her lip.

"But that's the problem, isn't it?" Pirate said, surprising them.

He was growing up.

28

May 31, 2024

Friday

"Their heads will all be up and happy." Miranda watered the plants at the schools, bushes she had placed in front of the buildings.

Harry and Susan, who had come for a last-minute check, stopped to admire Miranda's work. "When did your schools get indoor plumbing, water?" Susan asked.

"Oh, it came in stages, if my memory serves me. Given the creek is strong running, carrying water was part of studying here. We had pipes before they did." Miranda smiled. "My parents said work here was done in stages. First a well was dug, the usual, then lines were put into each building, and each had an outdoor pump. No faucets inside. By the time I was in grade school, they had everything. But, remember, these improvements were even slow with the white schools."

"Not the private, I bet." Harry stared at a fresh pansy face looking right back at her.

"Of course." A truck rumbled by. "I have been here since nine this morning. One delivery after another. But give the boys credit, the food tables, the lectern, they're all arranged. This must be the chairs."

"It better be." Susan, thrilled though she was, also wanted the celebration to be over.

"It is. There's Lucas." Harry watched the blond fellow cut the motor and hop out of the rented truck.

The other door opened. It was Paul, Tazio's husband.

"Where's Taz?" Susan wondered.

Miranda stepped toward the peonies she had planted. "She was here even before I arrived. Left before you got here, to pick up a lamp for the lectern. She said shadows might fall over it and that would make it hard for someone to read if their eyesight is not great."

"What a nice way to say if someone is old." Susan put her hands together in a silent clap.

"The only people under eighty giving speeches will be Tazio, making introductions, and Jim Sanburne, making a brief statement as mayor." Harry felt drops on her left leg.

"Sorry." Miranda apologized.

"I'm not sugar. I won't melt."

"These nozzles that you can twist, I have to fool with them. Have the right wide spray now, and you've proven that." Miranda pretended to aim for Harry.

"I was thinking, Jim is eighty, isn't he?" Harry moved a little farther back. "He has to be. I don't know why but I rarely think of anyone's exact age, including my own."

"Wise." Miranda laughed at her. "Creeps up on you."

"We'll have a fair number of kids tomorrow. They're all hoping to get older. The years drag when you're a kid. Everyone seems to be bigger than you." Susan watched as the two men assembled the chairs into rows. "I hope Tazio has the reserve ribbons and signs in her car."

"She will. Tazio redefines *organization*."

They watched Lucas and Paul, heard the faint click when the folding chairs were opened.

"Do you think we should put some in the back? I never thought of that," Harry said, worried.

Susan responded, "I did. I figured if people had folding chairs in their trucks and cars, they could get them should a baseball or football game start up."

"Do you think people will think of that?" Miranda finished her watering.

"If they don't, they can always walk up front and snag chairs after the speeches. And we'll have a few in the gym. Also, Lucas and Paul will pull the bleachers out. The people selling things can use them. They were told to set up after noon. There'd just be too much confusion to have everything going at once," Harry replied. "We've got quilters, an equine jeweler, T-shirts, and caps, of course. And Bluebird will have books for sale. Susan, what do we have, about fifteen vendors?"

"Yes. The sneaker store came in at the last minute."

"Should be cool in the gym," Miranda stated. "When will the tents arrive? As I recall last we spoke, you said you had tents."

Harry checked her watch. "They should be getting here soon. Tell you what, the tents are expensive, but we've got to have them. Actually, Miranda, it's supposed to be warmer tomorrow, mid-seventies and sunny. We'll need the tents. Who's to say a last-minute storm won't roll in? You never know. Susan, let's check the gym before everyone starts setting up."

"Miranda, this is perfect." Susan gave the older woman a kiss on the cheek.

Harry kissed the other one.

Tazio rolled down the road, pulled up. They told her where they were heading. She paused a few moments to catch up with Miranda, then she, too, headed for the gym.

Once inside, the three women found Fair and Ned, ladders against the walls, hanging up the name plaques. They had been there since seven in the morning.

"Oh my God, they really look fabulous!" Tazio exclaimed, as the Charleston green, four-feet-by-three-feet signs were affixed to the walls. The gold names glittered.

Not two minutes later, Lucas and Paul walked in.

"You all need to double-check the chairs, the lectern." Calling up to Fair, Lucas said, "We can help with this. Will go faster."

"Sure," Fair agreed. "Course, we've done most of the work."

"Right." Paul smiled. "We'll be back. Come on, ladies."

The three women and two men returned to the front of the schools. Everyone agreed it was as it should be.

"Let me hook up the lamp." Tazio opened the door to her truck, which was parked in front of the grade school, and pulled out the brass lamp. Holding it up, she said, "Batteries. Just in case."

"Let's do this together." Paul took the lamp.

"It's not that hard," she said.

"I know. Two minutes, then back to the gym."

Harry and Susan walked in. The gym door was open, and they stopped a moment to admire the floors.

"As soon as the boys are done, I'll mop this up," Harry volunteered. "I doubt the vendors will make a mess."

Once Paul returned, the four men got to work on the wooden nameplates.

"If one of us holds the ladder, then one man each can steady the bottom of the nameplates. That way, two can go up at a time," Harry suggested.

"Okay. Everything is measured out. You can see it. We put small marks on the walls," Fair told them.

"The other wall is already done. I had no idea how that would change this room," Susan remarked.

With extra hands, the job took only an hour.

A truck passing behind them caught everyone's attention.

"Who is driving in the back?" Lucas trotted to the open door. "You won't believe this."

They all hurried to him.

"Arch Munson. Come on." Fair led the way as Arch and his three sons and one grandson, jammed in his truck, were already unloading bleachers for the baseball diamond.

"What the hell!" Ned grabbed an end of a bleacher next to Arch's grandson.

"Talked to Moz. I remember playing on this field and now it's looking like back in the day. Come on, boys," he called to his sons, as burly as their father. "So I decided we need the bleachers."

"I can't believe you've done this, Arch." Tazio got a little teary.

"You know, all the work you put into this while the rest of us watched, this is the least I can do. The times we had back here." He got a little misty himself. "I've even got bats, gloves, balls. Called some of the old players, not many of us left, told them to get their asses here after the dedication. We're going to play some ball."

Amid laughter, memories, the group, with the women watching, put those bleachers up. The three women knew they could have helped, but also knew they should let the men do it. The fellows wanted a female audience, most men do, and after all was in place, they glowed at the praise.

The rest of the day was busy, and a few odd traffic jams or difficulty unloading stuff kept them moving.

Armand supervised the caterer, who came to see where he should put his truck. Harry, who had figured out parking with Fair and Susan, gave orders and felt it should be quietly set up once the speeches started. When done, people would have to get their food and carry it to the tables, but it should work, as the tables weren't far.

"Lot going on," Armand said.

They stood there, Fair and Ned joining them.

"Armand, you should go see the nameplates in the gym," Fair told him.

"I'll see them tomorrow. Need to get back to work. Fridays and Mondays are always the worst."

"How's business?" Paul asked.

"Well, it depends on which part of the world you're dealing with. Europe, pretty good, despite all. Russia goes up and down. The Middle East is losing people, losing money in America. We're okay. Could be better, but I've seen it worse."

"True," Fair agreed. "Well, do try to get in there tomorrow. You'll be in the middle of the vendors. We have stuff you might want and stuff you won't. The crystal company, I forget the name, they'll be there, and quilters, clothes, antiques."

Armand smiled. "I promise to see it all."

The restoration group worked until sundown. Exhausted, they finally left.

Once at home, slumped at the kitchen table, Harry opened her eyes wide. "Did I forget to lock the buildings?"

"No. You locked the schools. Lucas locked the gym. You'll fret yourself into a headache." Fair patted her hand. "I'll make tea."

"You should be exhausted, having put up all those heavy wooden plaques."

"Had help. We both need a good night's rest."

"Not before giving me treats," Pewter insisted.

Fair listened to the meow, opened the cabinet, pulled out goodies, and gave everyone a bacon bit or a handful of crunchies in their bowl.

As he then boiled water, Harry watched. "It's finally hitting me that this is it. After tomorrow, we'll be done. Well, Jim will need to find someone to supervise the place, of course, but we're done."

"A period at the end of the sentence."

"That is one way to put it." She took her teacup in hand.

"I suppose we're all feeling this."

She took a restorative sip. "Yes. You know what else occurs to me? Will Sandy's killer be there? I believe it's someone close."

"Honey, don't dwell on it. Get a good night's sleep. Tomorrow will be a wonderful day. Little things will go wrong. They always do. My prediction is people will get stuck parking. But tomorrow will be unforgettable."

"Well."

"Enjoy our victory."

29

June 1, 2024

Saturday

The day of the reunion had finally arrived. The temperature at sixty-eight degrees, twinned with forty-seven percent humidity, tickled each breath. The air slid down Harry's throat, feeling cold and energizing. The sky, a deep blue, deeper than robin's-egg blue, hosted enormous, impressive white cumulus clouds.

Fair drove the dually, the two cats and two dogs in the backseat.

"Can you believe we've got this fabulous day?" Harry looked up at the sky through the front windshield.

"Shouldn't warm up too much. Everyone's prayers are answered."

"That's the truth," she agreed.

"Honey, I'm going to park in the lot. But I can drop you right at the school buildings so you don't have to walk."

"I don't mind. A little walk will rev my motor."

"Since when do you need your motor revved?" He laughed at her.

Early as they were, when Fair pulled into the parking area, there were already thirty cars and trucks.

"Great day." Harry echoed what her grandmother used to say.

"I think it's going to be just that." Fair parked up on higher ground, right by the front. "Maybe some of these are vendors' cars."

"Could be, but everyone, with few exceptions, set up last night. Everything is ready to go. The only activity that will happen apart from the speeches is the people going to the tables with their food. And the food won't be put out until the last of the speeches." Harry added, "Armand has all arranged so there's no rustling or moving during the dedication."

"Paying for the caterer was a great gift." Fair stopped, cut the motor.

"It was. And it's food everyone likes. Hamburgers, hot dogs, chicken fingers, mac and cheese, salad. Nothing that will spill all over you. No fried chicken. Much as I like it, eating it creates a mess."

"Yes, it does." He smiled. "Too bad we couldn't have chickens in the back of the buildings. The students did."

"If we had a nice chicken coop, how long before we had owls swooping down, even with a cover? Chicken wire helps. But then come the foxes and the coyotes. You and I can have chickens at home because we're there. This place won't have people in it around the clock. Would be good for the students though."

"Honey, I'm not so sure of that, but it's a topic for another day. Hey, forgot to tell you. Did you know the name of the crystal seller's booth is Hot Rocks?"

She started laughing. "Too good!" Paused. "Oh, someone will have a fit."

He laughed, as well. "If they do, it's on them. No sense of humor."

Harry, Fair, Mrs. Murphy, Pewter, Tucker, and Pirate walked to the school buildings. Harry had a key that fit all the doors, the same locks that had always been there, plus a modern lock just to be safe.

"Susan's late," Harry said without emotion, just a fact.

"No, I'm not," came a voice behind her. "I was over in the gym with Tazio."

Harry and Fair turned. "Hi."

"This is going to be some day." Susan glowed. "Most of the vendors are already at the tables. I emphasized no selling during the speeches. They're good with that. But you know what? Why didn't I think of this? There have been some visitors prowling behind the gym. It's gruesome."

"Terrible things fascinate people," Harry bluntly said. "Come on, Susan, let's check each building." She kissed her husband on the cheek. "Love you. See you and Ned at the speeches."

"Will do." Fair headed toward the speaking area. He wanted to check the waste cans, make sure there were rows wide enough for the disabled and they were clearly marked.

Harry opened the grade school building. The women and animals stepped inside.

"Don't turn on any lights, Harry. We don't want people in here until after the speeches. Our idea to start with the speeches was good. Then everyone has the rest of the day to wander about, buy stuff, and, who knows, maybe play baseball."

"I hope so. Usually speeches start after people have wandered about. But then, the distances aren't too close. We'd have people running for their seats once the band stops. Should be thrilling."

"Did you bring any cash?" Susan asked.

"I did. Do you need some?"

"No. I didn't want to carry a purse so I wore my old summer skirt with the deep pockets. Have my cash, one credit card, and glasses inside."

Harry knew the skirt. "Kills me that most skirts aren't made with pockets. That's why I am wearing my khakis. I don't look fancy, but I'm clean. Have my keys in my right pocket and cash in the left. But will we get time to buy anything?"

"Maybe we will." Susan checked the back door. "Let's leave this locked. Everything looks good. Putting a lesson plan on each teacher's desk, clever. I wonder who will read them?" Susan double-checked the old paper on the desks with a paperweight on top.

"The handwriting is so lovely. People really could write then. Penmanship was a big deal."

"You have good handwriting," Susan complimented her.

"Thanks, but it's nothing like my mother's or your mother's."

"In a class by themselves. Let's go to the next building." They walked into the refreshing air, sweet, a light breeze now. Harry locked the front door.

Susan took out her identical key to open the high school building. "Oh, don't all those books in the bookcase look perfect? Right from the different decades. Jerry Showalter worked a miracle getting this stuff, investigating what was taught, and popular then for reading."

Harry walked in front of the bookcase, while the cats headed for the mouse hole. "Literacy is the key to power, if you think about it. Most all leaders, whether ancient or modern, are well-read. A few Western leaders couldn't read, but most could. Think of all the languages the first Queen Elizabeth knew. Or Edward I, back in the thirteenth century. Latin, English, and mostly French. Well educated. I would kill to see the Library of Alexandria. What a loss when it was destroyed."

"Funny, I never thought if that's true for, say, the Chinese or Japanese cultures. Or the Mideast."

"Susan, you know the emperors could read, plus think of all the servants they had. As for the Middle East. Alexandria. Even before Alexandria. Think of the hieroglyphics."

Susan smiled. "I don't believe there are any books on hieroglyphics here."

"All right, all right." Harry flicked Susan's shoulder with her middle finger, a thunk.

"I know you're in there," Pewter cooed.

"So," a squeak replied.

"Be people in and out of here," Mrs. Murphy informed the mouse. *"You and your friends might want to keep out of sight. No pooping on the floor while we're gone either."*

A discussion could be heard, then a lone voice called out, "*Okay.*"

"Looks good. I'm leaning a cricket bat against the teacher's desk." Susan opened the closet, retrieving the formidable bat. "There."

"Do you want to be in this building or the grade school building?" Harry asked.

"Grade school. But if someone else wants to be inside there, that's okay. I like showing the textbooks and also I want to be out of the crowd."

"Sounds good."

They left the high school building, locked the doors, and walked to the speech area, both taking seats off to the side, where the restoration committee would sit. They could see Armand with the caterers, the big truck off to the side of the event. The small tables for people to sit at had been set out on the other side of the truck. Best to have people eat in the shade, and those trees had lived for close to a century and a half, a few even more. It was a delightful place to have an outdoor lunch.

"Ah, here comes Aunt Tally." Harry and Susan stood while Teresa and Lucas put Aunt Tally at the end of the restoration row. The group thought she would get bumped about if she sat or was at the end of a row with the rest of the people.

"Ready?"

"Yes," the two answered in unison.

People began to fill up the seats. They could hear the high school band marching toward them. Soon people were standing in the aisles while others sat, for everyone wanted to hear the band. The kids looked wonderful and played great. As they continued, the speakers walked from the gym. Nobody really noticed them until they stood behind the podium, then all sat down. Finally, the band ended by playing the school's alma mater, which was a rendition of "Flow Gently, Sweet Afton." All the graduates, including the speakers, stood, singing the words.

The band then repaired to seats specially set for them, a placard announcing the same. The organizers wanted to make sure every young person was able to get a lot to eat. They could carry their instruments to the tables in the shade when the time came.

As the music and the singing faded away, Jim Sanburne stood at the podium. He welcomed everybody, identifying himself as the mayor of Crozet. He kept it short. Gave a brief rendition of the history of Crozet, originally known as Wayland's Crossing during colonial times. He then praised the restoration committee and ended with, "These findings, the restoration, will I hope provide us reason to keep searching our history. As your mayor for forty years, I thank you for putting your trust in me. Our once little hamlet has grown, but sensibly so. Newcomers quickly become neighbors. We will all build toward the future together."

He sat down to applause.

"Who put the history of the schools on the seats? I didn't see anyone do it," Harry whispered.

"Armand. Once he got the caterer organized, he asked Tazio what was left. She handed him a pile of booklets. They both did it really. Very nice pamphlet, by the way," Lucas filled them in.

Next up was Tazio, who provided a brief history of the physical restoration, adding that she hoped this would be a community resource as well as a teaching tool for students in Albemarle County. She named her co-workers on the committee. Each person stood to applause then sat down with relief.

Next was Norton Sessions, wearing the apparel of his Cherokee people. He explained how Walter Plecker pushed Black people and Native peoples together, pigeonholing them under the same classification, and all the ways it harmed them. He held the booklet, advising them to read it for more information, as all the Native American tribes local to the area were specifically mentioned. The teachers, he said, led them through the difficult times with such grace. He credited his starting his car-repair business to the discipline he had to learn here. "Our teachers expected a lot of us. We rose to the occasion. I will always be grateful to the friends I made here and to my teachers."

Next up was Evie Rogers, the valedictorian of the class of 1959. Dynamic, clearheaded, she remembered being dismissed by others because she was a girl and because she was Black. Her mother told her the only person who can bring you down is yourself. Believe in yourself. She did. She recalled how she and Sherry Tutweiler, now Evenfall, decided to become History teachers. By the time they graduated from college, the segregated schools had been closed. They continued to study. She wound up teaching History at Alabama State. Sherry broke barriers and taught at Charlottesville High School and later at the then new junior college. Sherry married Coach Evenfall. Evie paused, then said she was sure that Sherry is the reason Coach won everything. Made people laugh. Evie recalled the hard times without rancor. She ended with "The past is prologue. Learn history."

She left the podium to cheers. Then Coach got up. He looked over the audience. He told them how thrilled he was that so many graduates had come, that so many were still alive. Then he launched into, "I may give out but I won't give up. I impressed this on the boys. We went up against good coaches, good teams. Those were hard-fought games, no matter the sport." He called out his players sitting in the chairs. And he kindly remembered Tillie Fountain, one of the best athletes he had ever seen. He told the story about Tillie's sixty-yard pass and recalled there was nothing he could do for her. He couldn't use a girl on any team. But she went on to be a golf pro, dying young from breast cancer. He then slid into taking care of yourself. The cures for cancer just weren't there in Tillie's time. Today she would be alive. He urged the audience to get checkups, not to hide from their problems but face them head-on, whether physical or emotional. Never give up!

After Moz said "Never give up," he paused. The crowd cheered. Then, broad smile, he said, in his rich, deep voice, "All these years, all through Virginia, we have been burdened with Walter Ashby Plecker's entrenched racism, how he perpetuated segregation and encouraged the use of the term 'colored.' Of course, when students visit here in coming years, they will be taught about that, just as they will need to be taught how to properly start a woodburning stove." Many in the audience smiled, happy to think of the young learning about physical reality. "Those of us who were affected, the last graduates from the high school, are old now. We remain grateful to our teachers. To honor the progress that has been made, we would like to change the name of the Colored Schools, and we have selected Miss Letitia Small as the person whom we want to name them after. She took over in the 1930s. Was old when I studied. Age did not soften her determination to do the best for us. If she wasn't rapping her ruler on her desk to get students' attention, she was down at the County Commission meetings to push for newer textbooks, to argue for additions to the library. Her students were always on her mind. She left this earth in 1962, but she never truly left us. I've remembered. I'm grateful. We want Miss Small to be remembered as long as there is a Crozet." He turned, gesturing toward the school buildings behind him, where four men held up a beautiful painted sign. "Letitia Small Schools." He sat down.

A moment of silence was shattered by a roar of approval. Many in the audience shed tears, most especially those who had known the formidable lady.

Aunt Tally wept so hard that Lucas held one of her hands; Teresa, the other.

Harry thought how Moz could motivate people. No wonder his boys won. They won to please him and they won because they believed in themselves.

People continued to cheer. Moz had tears running down his face, as well.

After the speeches, people rushed to the speakers, and the graduates who hadn't time to find one another earlier did. Many of the graduates, now in their eighties and nineties, walked up to Aunt Tally. Wonderful reunions. Aunt Tally usually attended the baseball and football games, as did much of Crozet. They laughed, remembering people, the music they'd loved, and how others, such as

Godfrey Cambridge and Flip Wilson, never got credit for bringing folks together. A lot of the talk was about finding the common thread.

Aunt Tally, enlivened, wanted to get out of her wheelchair. Teresa and Lucas helped to keep her in it.

Sherry came over, bringing Ashley with her.

"I hoped you'd be here," Lucas mentioned. "I'm sorry I couldn't get time with you before this. We've all been crazy. Your uncle's speech was fabulous." Then he looked at Sherry. "I'm not going to say my uncle-in-law or great-uncle-in-law."

They all laughed.

Harry left the group, hurried to grab two plates, loaded them up, and walked to the high school building. After putting the plates on the grass, she unlocked the door.

"About time," Pewter fussed.

Harry took the plates, dividing one up for the animals. She'd left a bowl in the building, and she now refilled it with water then sat at a desk to hurriedly eat two hot dogs and a big scoop of mac and cheese. A Co-Cola finished the repast.

Susan waved as she hurried to the grade school building.

After a deep breath, Harry stood up, gathered her debris, putting it in a paper bag, which she then put in the big wastebasket lined with a garbage bag.

She opened the door and people soon began to file in. The cats looked regal on the teacher's desk. Pirate sat behind it, as Harry asked him to. He could scare people with his size. Tucker greeted everyone.

Harry gave a good account of what a school day had looked like. What the young people had studied. She pointed out the inkwells, textbooks, and she mentioned that each row had books from a different decade. She noted how worn those books were, as these schools were at the end of the line. She pointed out the library and showed them the wooden box still containing library cards, using the Dewey Decimal System. She answered questions about heat, about fans in warm weather once electricity was installed. The basic facts riveted people. Where were the bathrooms? Originally outside. How did they see in winter's early darkness? She held up an empty whale oil lamp and showed them the places such lamps had been hung. She spoke of how at the end of every school day the students had to sweep down the room. In winter, the teachers arrived early to fire up the stove so when the students came in, the room would be warm. She also told them the students had to clean the windows in good weather. Some inside, some outside, cleaning together. Everything sparkled.

She mentioned where the barn used to be. Where hay was stored, and she encouraged them to visit the gym. Everyone could squeeze into the gym, grade school, and high school.

Pewter hopped off the desk, walking to the mouse quarters. She beheld a glittering pair of eyes.

"How long is this going to last?" the mouse asked.

"I don't know." Pewter was bored, she hoped it would end soon.

Harry was feeling the same. She wanted to go to the gym. Tempting as it would be to leave the building open, she felt she couldn't do that unless someone else was inside. The old books had some value, but more than that, she just didn't want people roaming about. So she gave everyone who came through the doors a tour. The most fun was when the old graduates came, and they showed her where they had sat, funny things that had happened. That made it all worthwhile.

Time passed, and finally no one came through. Harry checked her watch. She was hoping to get to the gym to buy a few things from the vendors. They could sell until six PM, but she worried that a few who'd traveled far would leave early. When she'd popped her head in before the speakers, she'd seen a pretty throw she wanted for the couch. Finally, she petted her friends, praising how good they were, then walked to the big windows. The coast looked clear.

"All right, guys, come on. Stick with me. I left leashes in the closet, just in case." She opened the closet and wrapped the leashes around her waist. "Okay."

Walking out into the late afternoon, the day still beautiful, perked her up. She was a little tired, and some of that was emotional. This had been a big day, and a long day.

Walking into the gym, she saw the place was packed. Many of the graduates and their children and grandchildren, even a few great-great-grandchildren, looked for their family names on the plaques. Vendors were doing a brisk business.

"There's no food in here," Pewter complained.

"There's an ice-cream stand." Pirate could see over the cats' heads, the stand being at the end of the line of vendors on one side.

"They don't have flavored ice cream," Pewter dismissed the idea.

"I like vanilla." Mrs. Murphy loved ice cream. *"Mom's going for the T-shirts. She has too many."*

Sure enough, Harry bought T-shirts for Fair, Susan, Ned, Lucas, Tazio, and even Aunt Tally. Then she carried her shopping bag, which came with the T-shirts, to the bookstore booth. She ordered books, as Bluebird was good about getting anything she wanted that was not on the shelf. After a long chat, she walked to the quilters.

"This stuff is clever. The designs really get you."

"Who cares about design? Is it warm?" Pewter was getting testy.

"She's going to talk to every vendor. Thank them for helping make the day special. Either we tag along or go under the bleachers." Tucker was accurate about Harry's working the room.

Lucas and Ashley stood at the booth where small, amusing wooden statues had been carved. There were elephants, cats, dogs, even a mule with painted spectacles. An owl with big eyes perched over a carved fox carrying a book.

"Clever," Harry remarked.

"What should I get for Aunt Tally? Teresa took her home. All this activity, people she hadn't seen for years, wore her out," Lucas informed Harry.

"She had the time of her life." Ashley picked up the owl. "Sacred to Athena."

Harry touched the table. "You know about the goddess?"

Ashley smiled. "I come from a long line of History teachers. I really had no choice. Sherry deserves this."

"Then you deserve Puss in Boots. That's such a good story." Lucas selected a wonderful carving of the famous cat.

"Hey." Harry caught Pewter as she jumped on the table, carefully setting her back on the floor. "You know better than that."

"I want to see Puss in Boots." The gray cat wiggled, ready to jump again.

Harry grabbed her, holding her in her arms. "She's interested in your carvings."

The lady behind the booth agreed. "Cats have good taste."

"See." Pewter smugly turned to face Harry.

The other three, at Harry's feet, watched, wondering what Pewter would get away with.

"Aunt Tally?" Lucas again questioned.

Harry picked up the fox he'd pointed to. "She'll like this." Then she picked up another carved cat. "This is for my cat, as well as Puss in Boots."

It was a copy of an ancient Egyptian cat.

"Don't let it go to your head, Pewter," Tucker grumbled. Harry then selected two dogs for Tucker and Pirate. They were delightfully goofy-looking.

"Think you'll participate in whatever game the guys decide to play?" Harry asked Lucas.

"Since those stands were delivered, I'll sit in them. Want to watch a game, Ashley?"

"If Moz is playing or coaching, you bet. Those bleachers will be full," she answered him.

"All right. Need to hit up the other booths." Harry disengaged, having dropped the carvings into her shopping bag, already starting to sag a little bit.

"There's some good stuff." Lucas pointed toward Hot Rocks.

Ashley tilted her head, a devilish look in her eye. "You know, he has a sense of humor, that guy."

The man in question was perhaps in his sixties, sporting a tidy gray goatee. The display drew people, as many of the crystals had been split open to reveal the dazzling insides. Armand was in discussion with Riley Ott, the owner. Harry, along with another woman, paused at a huge amethyst.

"I think this is majestic. So big," the lady enthused.

"It is. Makes me understand why some people are miners. I suppose even coal can be fascinating," Harry responded.

"Anything profitable is fascinating," the lady replied.

"Ladies. Oh, hello, Harry. I'm keeping you from Mr. Ott. There's a lot to buy." Armand smiled.

Harry lifted a big chunk of bluestone while the other woman engaged Mr. Ott. "This reminds me of what I picked up, I love the flecks, like in mica."

Armand took the stone from her hand. "It is pretty."

Mr. Ott, having sold the smaller amethyst geode to the lady, walked behind his desk, looking over at them. "Kyanite. Has wonderful heat properties, can withstand so much. It's used in ceramics, where you would expect its use, and it can also work in rocket heads. Has amazing properties."

Harry took the piece he handed her. "This is green."

Mr. Ott replied, "There is some green kyanite. The largest deposits that we know of in our country are down in Dillwyn. Of course, we have so much shale, too. Those Blue Ridge Mountains gave us all manner of riches. There're treasures still to be unearthed."

Armand took the piece from Harry as she offered it to him, mentioning, "Isn't that why Hades is the richest god? His kingdom is under the earth. All gold, silver, coal; everything is his."

"Yes." Harry noticed a large, perfect quartz crystal that was a foot long. "That's impressive." Then she turned to Armand. "You're the second person today I've heard mention a Greek god."

He shrugged. "Great stories."

Mr. Ott, happy to talk about the rocks, crystals, his wares, said, "The Russians would kill to have our kyanite. They have some, but just a little. We're like the South Africans with aluminum. We have so much."

"So is it a national treasure? Would kyanite be considered an ore, a stone of national security?" Harry asked.

Armand piped up. "Probably, but how are they going to get any of it?" He gave the green kyanite back to her.

"Hey," she opened her mouth and spoke without thinking, "Sandy was fluent in Russian. Maybe that's where the money was really coming from."

Armand paused. "I suppose we can speculate about anything."

Mr. Ott, who had read about Sandy Rycroft's death, let Harry drop the green kyanite into his hands. "Even though there was yellow tape behind the buildings earlier, people trooped back there. Who knows, maybe something turned up, but you'd think they'd stay away. That's why the yellow tape was put up."

"As I worked with him from time to time, I guess I do hope someone finds something. I've known Sandy's family for years. So far nothing," Armand told Mr. Ott. "And this young lady found him."

Harry didn't want to elaborate. "It was a great shock."

"I bet it was. When I saw it on the news, I thought he must have known the killer. Why else would he be here? He wasn't driven somewhere distant. So I think it was spur of the moment. Excuse me." Mr. Ott broke off to help another customer.

Hot Rocks's business was booming.

"Come on, babydolls." Harry clicked her fingers.

As she walked, stopping at more booths, Armand caught up with her, excusing himself from further discussion with Mr. Ott. "The game should start soon."

"Are you going to play?" Pirate stuck close to Harry as she walked.

"Yes. My gear is in the car. You know, I didn't get the tour of the high school. Too busy with the caterers. The high school is on my way to the parking lot. Will you give me a tour?"

"Of course." Harry couldn't really refuse the man who'd paid for the food. They reached the front door, she unlocked it, and they stepped inside.

"It's not too hot in here. I think the temperature is now in the mid-seventies," he noted.

"It's the shade. They were smart when they sited these buildings. The trees were big then. And look at them now."

"I'm going to visit our mouse." Pewter trotted to the school desk.

"I'll go with you." Mrs. Murphy walked beside her.

A roar went up.

"The game's started. Let me hurry up." Harry wanted to see a bit of the game herself.

"Don't worry about it. Were you coming to do more cleaning or work the day you found Sandy?"

"I was. Here's the potbellied stove. Works like a treat."

"Did he say anything to you?"

"Armand, what has that to do with the tour?"

"Trying to piece it together. He'd been upset. Not reliable."

"I wouldn't know. When I got to him, he was dying." Harry began to get a prickly feeling. "I know before that day he wasn't happy about the GPR. We didn't discuss it in detail though." She thought a moment, then blurted, "Armand, you were his silent investor, weren't you?"

A long pause followed, then he said, "I had funds prepared."

"For international stakeholders?"

"Oh, Harry, you are smart." Armand sighed. He sounded resigned. "I am just now realizing how smart. Yes. It is worth billions. Hard to believe, but millions is nothing when you own something that's very rare: gold, silver, aluminum, kyanite."

"Kyanite?" She echoed his word. "So it's not shale?"

"Shale is valuable, but not that valuable."

"Why was Sandy upset?" she asked.

"He spoke to my Russian client. I thought he had lined up all the arrangements. To a point, he did, but then he lowballed the restoration committee. He could have offered much more for the land. I nailed him. He said why pay more than you had to? I said he was going to pocket extra savings. Since I don't speak Russian, I then knew I couldn't trust him."

"Ah."

"Slowly you are piecing it together. I can't take the chance. I want you to walk with me to my car. Best not stay here."

"And what if I refuse?" She glared at him, shocked but not paralyzed.

He pulled out a small pistol. "Who will hear it with the noise? Start walking."

"I'll bite his ankles. You push him down." Tucker lunged at Armand's ankles.

"Call off your dogs. I'll shoot them." Armand swung at the corgi.

"Tucker, Pirate. No." Harry slowly walked.

Pewter meowed at the mouse-door opening. *"Come out and chase the man."*

"How do I know you won't chase me?" came a squeak.

"I promise. Please. Our human is in danger."

The mouse popped out. Saw the man with the gun pointing at Harry's side. *"Death! Hellfire!"* came a mighty squeak.

"No!" Armand squealed, terrified of the mouse, too scared to fire.

"Get him," Harry ordered the dogs.

Pirate hit Armand, who was screaming in fear of the mouse, flooring him with all one hundred and fifty pounds of Irish Wolfhound muscle. Tucker grabbed Armand's wrist, bit as hard as she could, causing blood to spurt from the veins going to the hand. Armand dropped the gun.

Harry picked it up. The mouse circled Armand, who was now shaking like a leaf. Still, he tried to bolt for the door.

"Stop."

Armand didn't. Harry shot his left kneecap from behind. He dropped. She stood over him. "Next time it's your head."

"Don't shoot. Don't shoot." He grabbed his left leg, moaning in pain.

"You stabbed Sandy, didn't you?"

Armand didn't answer, so Harry clubbed him on his head with the gun. He nodded, indicating that he had.

Since Armand was down, Pewter took the opportunity to scratch the man's face. The mouse watched this with wonder.

"You did good," Pewter, puffed up from scratching Armand, praised the little creature.

"I'm going back to my house. Next time you come here, bring me treats."

"I promise." Pewter licked her paw, rubbed her face. She felt this was further humiliation for the killer.

"Good dogs. Good work. You too, Pewter and Mrs. Murphy." Harry held the gun on Armand, plucked her cellphone out of her back pocket, called Fair.

Fair, down at the baseball game waiting for her, heard the signal, put his phone to his ear, and heard, "I'm in the high school. I need help. If you see Cooper, bring her."

"Susan, Ned, come on." Fair motioned to Cooper, a few rows over.

Tazio and Paul started to get up, as did Lucas and Ashley.

Fair called over his shoulder. "Stay with the game. We'll take care of it."

Fair and Cooper ran faster than Susan and Ned. Seeing his wife standing over Armand, half in and half out of the front door of the high school building, he rushed to her. "Are you okay?"

"I am. He murdered Sandy."

Cooper immediately handcuffed him, ignoring his condition.

Armand was writhing in pain. Tucker and Pirate stood nearby, ready to attack if necessary.

Cooper called Sheriff Shaw, who fortunately was sitting at the

side of the road in front of the post office. That slowed traffic, as there were still so many people coming to the sound of the baseball game.

As Harry told Fair, Susan, Ned, and Cooper what had happened, Pewter boasted, "*I saved the day.*"

Tucker and Pirate remained silent.

Mrs. Murphy acknowledged her friend. "*Pewter scratched him. She had help from a mouse. The dogs got him down.*"

Sheriff Shaw arrived at the school. Harry, who had handed the gun to Coop, was still shaking.

Noticing, the sheriff said, "Come into the building. Sit down. Tell me what you know."

They all trooped into the building. Harry carefully started with meeting Armand in the gym. Susan ran out to get Harry a Co-Cola. Something to help steady her. Her dearest friend took the cold bottle and chugged it.

The others sat there, shocked, horrified. An ambulance came to pick up Armand. No one bothered to worry that he'd get away.

Cooper, seeing a crowd gathering outside the school building, said, "I'll go with the ambulance."

"Do. And Cooper, make sure he's under guard around the clock. I'm taking Harry's statement," Rick said.

Pirate sat by Harry, putting his head under her hand. Tucker leaned against her legs. Mrs. Murphy sprawled on the desk, patting Harry's hand with her paw.

Pewter sashayed to the mouse's entrance. "*You did good.*"

"*What fun to hear a big sissy scream.*" The little gray fellow giggled.

30

June 6, 2024

Thursday

Bitsy, on her back in Aunt Tally's lap, luxuriated in being stroked. Pewter took over the aged dachshund's bed on the floor while Mrs. Murphy, Tucker, and Pirate lay on the wonderfully faded Chinese rug. Aunt Tally loved old Chinese rugs. Harry, Fair, Susan, Ned, Lucas, and Cooper sat in her living room. The open window allowed the breeze to flow through and the mid-seventies temperature felt cooler with the breeze.

Aunt Tally wanted to celebrate D-Day, as well as hear what had happened with Armand, given all that'd had to be done, including getting Harry's shooting of Armand declared self-defense. This was the first time Aunt Tally had been able to get everyone together.

Cooper told her, "He's still in custody at the hospital. We put a twenty-four-hour guard on him. He can't get away with saying the painkillers confused him."

"Won't he admit anything?" Ned knew he hadn't so far. "But he can't wiggle free from pulling a gun on Harry, threatening to kidnap her, essentially."

"What about Sandy?" Susan had heard all this, but thought Aunt Tally would want the information.

"He's shut up about it, but of course Harry can testify as to what he said to her. It will take a good prosecutor, but I think we can put him away." Cooper actually felt positive about it, and she usually did not when it came to a courtroom.

"And his Russian connections?" Lucas wondered if the authorities knew who was paying the bills.

"There's nothing we can do to prove they fostered criminal behavior. We know the money came from a large mining company. That's pretty much it."

"So they must have highly trained geologists," Lucas said. "Like Denver Raiselle?"

"Yes." Cooper added, "Russia's government was in a different phase in 2006 when Raiselle disappeared. Was he part of the impending deal? Not a shred of proof. But I have found bills from 2004 and 2005 to Hickory Real Estate for soil testing. That will take more study from our department. All of this happened so fast. Armand took a stupid chance.

"Did the Russians know we have a large amount of kyanite, possibly the largest in the world? Yes. But so do every other country's geologists, at least now." Cooper sighed. "It is possible this planning to dominate a rare resource was two generations in the making. Our local focus is the murder. We can all hope Armand finally cites his fear or anger of Sandy."

"Kyanite has remarkable heat-resistance properties, which means it has military usage. Not that I ever knew of such a thing." Harry paused. "Until recently."

"In order to retrieve the ore—I think of it as an ore, you might think of it as a crystalline structure—a company would have to spend millions to create the purchase, buy equipment. So if they bought the land behind the schools, all of downtown Crozet would be disrupted forever." Cooper had done her research. "More than disruption, think of the noise."

"Yes, but we'd be getting millions yearly from taxes and probably from goodwill expenditures." Ned then hastily said, "Not that I'm in favor of it, but you can imagine the terrific fighting this would provoke."

"Don't you think most people would go for the money, especially as they would be getting a lot of it in one form or another? Think of the jobs it would create." Lucas held his palms upward. "I'm not saying Crozetians are greedy, but this would be a tremendous uplift financially, even as it would destroy some of the lovely countryside. Given the resident hardships, thanks to Covid and the high interest rates, inflation, maybe Armand wasn't so far off. People would have the money to move farther from town because a smart company would give them the choice."

"Greed." Susan inhaled. "Sometimes I think that's what makes the world go round, not love."

"Who knows?" Harry shrugged.

"You all are being defeatist, and on June 6th." Aunt Tally schooled them. "I was twenty-three on D-Day. Those people faced bigger problems than we have now."

"That's true, Aunt Tally." Lucas agreed with her. "But we knew one another better then. Just think of the drafts. Young men were thrown together with men from all different walks of life. And the boys from Ivy League colleges went into the service after Pearl Harbor. They didn't try to buy their way out. So many served. We learned about one another. Think of transportation. Not out here in the country, but in the cities. People rode the buses, you sat with people different from yourself. Now, I don't know." He paused.

Ned filled in the space. "Millions of people are living with people much like themselves. They don't have to learn about anyone else. I see this to some degree in the House of Delegates. But if we want to learn about one another, we will."

"But is learning respecting others?" Harry looked at him.

"I hope so," Aunt Tally piped up again. "I'm not giving up on my country. Yes, a terrible thing happened here, but not every resident of Crozet is a killer. We too often focus on the negative. But I still believe we can rise above it."

"You're right to correct us, Aunt Tally." Cooper smiled. "I see failures every day, whether it's failure of attention or a failure of ethics. But I want to believe we can improve. You give me heart."

Aunt Tally beamed, looking around at the gathering. "Think of the wonderful thing you did for all of us, the restoration of the schools. The dedication ceremony. Naming the schools after Letitia Small, who I adored. She was older than me, but I saw her so frequently in town. At the ceremony, I saw people I haven't seen in decades. What a great gift you all gave us. We can't let one or two bad doers spoil that. Plus, I heard Moz Evenfall hit a home run."

"He did." Fair grinned. "I was with Harry, but I heard the roar."

"It's a glorious day." Aunt Tally clapped her hands.

"Yes, it is." Susan noticed Teresa coming down the hall with drinks and Aunt Tally's famous corn bread. "Aunt Tally, you are spoiling us."

Teresa sat the tray on the big coffee table and started cutting pieces for everyone.

"Who would like spirits?" Aunt Tally asked.

"What a way to celebrate. I would." Lucas adored the old lady.

"Well, Lucas, you know where the bar is. Fix yourself a drink, and everyone else, too."

As Lucas took orders, Teresa put big slices of corn bread on small plates, along with a hunk of butter, a small knife, and a napkin. Harry took one, gave one to Susan, then put plates where the men were sitting. Cooper got the biggest piece of all, prompting Harry to tease her.

Sitting there, eating, drinking, recalling recent events both good and bad, Harry mentioned, "My grandfather was out to sea on D-Day. Most of you know he was the radio operator on a destroyer.

Anyway, here's to all our boys . . . and the girls in uniform, too." She lifted her glass of sherry, unusual for her.

"Hear, hear." They all toasted.

"*I want food.*" Pewter was not shy.

As it happened, Teresa, being well prepared, had a little cup of bits of last night's pork for the cats. There were bigger pieces for the dogs, especially Bitsy, who jumped off Aunt Tally's lap.

"*Yeah!*" came the animal chorus.

"You know what crosses my mind?" Harry had already polished off her corn bread.

"That's a frightening thought." Susan lifted one eyebrow.

"All right." Harry returned the look. "Today, June 6, was when Julius Caesar defeated Pompey the Great at Pharsalus in 48 BC. Maybe some days invite battles, others inspire operas. It's funny, if you look at history, how events, battles, or birthdays collide."

"Maybe so." Susan usually had a comeback. "When you're covering about two thousand years, there's bound to be similarities on the same day."

"I suppose. But these things wander in and out of my brain. Like Denver Raiselle. We'll probably never know the real reason for his demise. Did his knowledge threaten someone? Was he being asked questions that could jeopardize our national security? It was a different time then. Maybe he was a man who wasn't motivated by money. That would be suspicious to a lot of people, since so many believe everyone has a price. I don't know. But I think about it." Harry sipped the good sherry.

"Motive. If you have the motive, you're crossing home plate." Cooper put down her fork. "It may do you no good in a court of law, but it makes the crime understandable."

Lucas thought about this. "Yes, but understandable is not excusable. That gets me, making excuses for wrongdoing. It's used all the time to lighten or remove the consequences for crime."

"Given that I am the oldest person in the room, I can promise you that when actions do not have consequences, when you are not held to account, things go to hell in a hurry."

That got them going, all talking at once. Were there defensible crimes? What were they? The group enjoyed the discussion. It made everyone think.

"People waste a lot of time, don't they?" Pirate asked Tucker.

"Ideas. That kind of talk?" the smaller dog asked the big fellow.

"Why not deal with what's in front of you and not worry about what might be or not be? Who knows?" Pirate sat down.

"They love this stuff." Pewter snatched a piece of pork from Pirate's plate. *"I love this pork."*

"Whatever makes them or us happy. I do think we understand them better than they understand us, but that's okay. We can do so many things together with humans, like take walks, sit in front of the fire on a cold night, help them open packages." Mrs. Murphy liked opening packages; the crinkly paper was the best.

As the animals discussed the people, Harry held up her glass. "To my wonderful pets, who saved the day."

"Hear, hear," they called out again.

"And to the little mouse, God bless him. You know, I went back and put out cheese for him yesterday." Harry, grinning, held up her glass again.

All toasted the mouse.

"I was the one who got the mouse to run out," Pewter loudly meowed. *"Me."*

"Of course it was you." Mrs. Murphy leaned on the gray cat. *"We all know that. But, hey, she's doing the best she can."*

"It was you." Tucker followed Mrs. Murphy's lead. *"You saved Harry."*

Pewter lifted her head, purred. It was a perfect day.

ACKNOWLEDGMENTS

With thanks to Ivanka Perez and Katie Horn, my new team at Random House. Diane Harvey of Nelson County is a fountain of ideas and good humor.

Marianne Casey, MB and Russell Wagner have given me much to think about. What good minds they have.

Elinor Carrington Lyon continues to back me even though based in New York City. I owe her a great deal.

Lastly, my pair of tufted titmice greet me every morning, sometimes flying through the house if I leave the door open.

What a way to start the day.

AUTHOR'S NOTE

Little by little I have developed the story of restoring the schools. It has had a great impact on Virginia public education. Best we remember.

On a personal note, some of my horses have been with me almost forty years, longer than life with my parents. Only my school friends and church friends have been with me longer. Every year I love them more, both equine and human.

Mom always said, "It's your friends who get you through life."

Tell them you love them. For the horses, minty muffins help.

ABOUT THE AUTHORS

Rita Mae Brown has written many bestsellers and received two Emmy nominations. In addition to the Mrs. Murphy series, she has authored a dog series comprised of *A Nose for Justice* and *Murder Unleashed*, and the Sister Jane foxhunting series, among many other acclaimed books. She and Sneaky Pie live with several other rescued animals.

To inquire about booking Rita Mae Brown for a speaking engagement, please contact the Penguin Random House Speakers Bureau at speakers@penguinrandomhouse.com.

Sneaky Pie Brown, a tiger cat rescue, has written many mysteries—witness the list at the front of the novel. Having to share credit with the abovenamed human is a small irritant, but she manages it. Anything is better than typing, which is what "Big Brown" does for the series. Sneaky calls her human that name behind her back, after the wonderful Thoroughbred racehorse. As her human is rather small, it brings giggles to the other animals. Sneaky's main character—Mrs. Murphy, a tiger cat—is a bit sweeter than Miss Pie, who can be caustic.

ABOUT THE TYPE

This book was set in Joanna, a typeface designed in 1930 by Eric Gill (1882–1940). Named for his daughter, this face is based on designs originally cut by the sixteenth-century typefounder Robert Granjon (1513–89). With small, straight serifs and its simple elegance, this face is notably distinguished and versatile.